I0607958

Deliberate Deceptions

A Hauberk Protection novel

And

PERFECT PROPOSAL

A Hauberk Protection novella

by

LEAH BRAEMEL

DELIBERATE DECEPTIONS

A Hauberk Protection novel

LEAH BRAEMEL

DELIBERATE DECEPTIONS

She's guarding his body. He's guarding his heart.

Hostage negotiator Lauren Miller is used to staring danger in the face. Now a vengeful former team member is targeting her and anyone she cares about, including her ex-husband. Although hiding them both in the same remote safehouse is risky, the plan could provide her with the perfect opportunity to make amends with the one man who has her heart.

Building Hauberk Protection into a success is the only thing that's kept Chad sane since his marriage to Lauren ended. He loved her more than life itself and losing her left a hole that haunts him still. When he unexpectedly finds himself trapped with her, Chad can think of only one up-side—he can finally learn why she walked away without an explanation.

Except the heat that burns between them is turning their defenses to ash. As their passion rekindles, Lauren struggles to keep her focus, especially when she learns that Chad wasn't the only one being deceived. And that deception puts both their lives in jeopardy.

DEDICATION

To N and J, who shared their fears and grief with me to help bring Chad and Lauren's story alive.

CHAPTER ONE

EIGHT YEARS AGO

LIFE COULDN'T GET ANY BETTER. Chad Miller soaked in the sight of his baby daughter in her mother's arms. Even from where he stood in the doorway, he could see Emily's lips drawn into a bow, moving as if she was still suckling. The light from the bedside lamp limned Lauren, gilding her hair that spilled over her shoulder. Had any man ever been so lucky?

"Hey, babe," he said softly so he wouldn't disturb Emily.

Lauren turned her head and gave him a smile worthy of a Madonna. "I didn't hear you come in. Everything go okay?"

"It went down perfect. We got the guy." Pride swelled in him as she carefully placed Emily in her cradle beside their bed. "Got some other good news too. You're looking at the Bureau's newest Supervisory Special Agent."

With a squeak of joy, Lauren ran toward him, heedless of the way the light turned her nightgown transparent. His cock hardened as he watched the V of her legs open and close with each step she took. No, not a Madonna. A siren. With a body to tempt any man. Except he was the only man who got to explore her sensuality.

He wrapped his arms about her and held her tight. God, he was so lucky to have them both. "I love you, baby."

She pulled back and gave him a cocky grin. "That's just because you hope to get lucky tonight."

"I'm lucky every night. Ever since you came into my life."

"I love you too. And I'm so proud of you." She kissed him, her lips soft on his, her tongue demanding entrance. He drew a deep breath, reveling in the lingering scent of Lauren's shampoo mixed with a hint of the baby powder she'd used on Emily. Her pelvis ground against his erection until he broke off the kiss with a groan.

Okay, so life could get better in one way. He glanced at the cradle as he stroked Lauren's behind, trailing one finger down the cleft in the center. "Emily asleep?"

"Mmm-hmm." The edges of Lauren's eyes crinkled with her smile. She pulled back to look at him, the warm brown irises glowing like a twenty-year-old scotch in the dim light. Then he noticed the dark circles beneath them.

With a frown, he rubbed a thumb over her jaw, loving how she rested her cheek in his palm. "You're tired, babe. Why don't we arrange a babysitter for tomorrow night? Go out. Indulge in some grown-up games for a change."

His balls ached at the thought that he'd not be able to celebrate right damned then. He'd been halfhard ever since the take-down. The adrenaline hadn't eased since he'd received news of his promotion and he'd been looking forward to this all night.

She cast a glance of her own at the cradle. "I'm all right, as long as we can be where I can keep an eye on her." Her hand drifted down his abdomen to smooth the fabric straining over his erection. The tiny dimple that only appeared on the right side of her smile deepened. "Besides, I think we need to take care of this bad boy soon or you're not going to sleep tonight."

"Not without a hand job in the shower." He released a slow breath when she unzipped his fly and stroked his cock. His fingers threaded through her hair, loving the feel of the silken strands against his skin. "Hell, you keep that up, I'm going to come right here."

With another hmm, Lauren sank to her knees. Two seconds later, his pants were around his ankles, his cock bobbing inches away from her face.

Warm breath was quickly followed by the moist heat of her mouth as she licked his crown. Her lips closed around his shaft in one swallow, wrenching a groan from him. They'd been together long enough they didn't need words; she knew instinctively what he liked. He tightened his grip on her hair when she cupped his balls, causing a familiar tingle at the base of his spine.

An animal-like growl rose in his throat as his seed pulsed into the warmth of her mouth. The sensation of her swallowing it around his cock nearly had his knees buckling. Her tongue swiped around the head, licking the last drops of his come as delicately as a cat licking the last of a bowl of cream. She sat back on her heels with a look of satisfaction.

"Come here, babe. Let me take care of you now." He pulled her to her feet and caressed her mound. His fingers parted her soft folds, sliding through the moisture.

She buried her face in the crook of his neck, her hips undulating her clit against his fingers. "It's all right, don't worry about me."

The hell with that. He walked her backward until the back of her knees hit the bed. Her head turned, seeking the cradle, but he captured her lips with his. "She's fine."

Once Lauren was horizontal, he banded her wrists and hauled them above her head. "Don't move."

She started to argue but he kissed her again, cutting off whatever she was about to say. They were both breathless by the time he pulled away. "Don't. Move."

He left her there while he opened the bedside table and chose a set of leather wrist restraints. It had been almost a year since he'd let himself take her the way he liked, the way she liked. Since Lauren had first told him she suspected she might be pregnant. He'd been gentle each time they'd made love, ensuring nothing he did would harm her or their baby. But tonight. Tonight there were no excuses not to indulge themselves.

Without being asked, she held up her hands. He kissed the tender skin on the inside of her wrists before he fastened the cuffs around them, then attached the restraints to the headboard. Free to explore at his leisure, he traced a finger around one areola. They were darker, bigger than they'd been before her pregnancy. God, he found it so amazing that she could give life to their child, and such pleasure to him.

Straddling her, he leaned down and kissed her mouth, pouring all the love she'd given him back to her. Beneath him, she shuddered, her hips undulating. His hand drifted over her belly, goose bumps raising wherever he touched. He slid his fingers between her creamy lips and plunged into her pussy. Lauren moaned into his mouth while grinding her clit against his palm.

He broke off the kiss. "Easy, babe. You'll get what you want in a minute."

His head dropped to her neck and he feathered kisses down her shoulder. He took his time, paying attention to her breasts, to her belly, to the silvery lines she'd worried made her look ugly. Would she ever believe him when he told her that he loved her stretch marks? That to him they were proof of the love they'd shared? Of their daughter.

He settled between her thighs. Her whole body trembled when his tongue touched her clit. His cock hardened, and his balls ached at the taste of her honey. He drove her up to the brink, backed off, then drove her up again until her juices coated his chin and she was begging him to let her come. His fingers working deep inside her, he lifted his head. Her cheek rested on the pillow, her shoulder-length hair a golden halo in the light. "Look at me, babe."

Her head turned as if it were a struggle to move. He watched her eyes unfocus as he sucked her clit. Her lips parted as she panted in short, hard bursts. He flicked his tongue against the nerve endings once, twice, with the strength he knew would tip her over the edge. The long expanse of her neck arched cutting off his view as her pussy spasmed around his fingers.

Before her muscles stopped their fluttering, he surged into her. Although they both tried to be quiet, he couldn't stop his groan. Damn, her pussy was still taut, clutching his cock with a welcoming warmth, the lingering remains of her orgasm driving him insane.

Lauren wrapped her legs around his waist and nailed his ass with her heels, pulling him even deeper. "Please," she whispered.

He closed his eyes and stopped moving, summoning his control over his need to plunge into her over and over, to use her hard and fast. He slid his hands beneath her silky, firm globes, adjusting the angle before withdrawing, inch by slow inch. Just as slowly as he'd withdrawn, he pressed back in, until she was whimpering, her body shaking with need.

No matter how rigid his control, soon he was flexing his hips until the bed frame bounced against the wall, burying every inch of himself into the most sublime place on earth. The sensation of her heated channel rippling tight around his cock shattered his restraint. His balls tight to his body, he buried his face between her breasts and let his need for Lauren, his pride and his love, pour into her.

His body sagged on her until he gathered the strength to roll over. He reached up and undid the restraints. As soon as she was free, Lauren curled inside his embrace. A breath, maybe two, and she was asleep, her lips parted, her eyelashes long on her cheeks.

He started to rouse her, wanting to take her again, but the circles beneath her eyes stopped him. Emily hadn't been waking for the two-o'clock feeding for a month now, but Lauren still seemed exhausted even though she usually managed at least six hours uninterrupted sleep most nights. He stroked her breast, thumbing the heavy nipple that beaded beneath his touch. Hell, he chastised himself, she was feeding a child, that would be enough to make anyone tired.

He glanced over Lauren's shoulder and saw the gentle rise and fall of Emily's chest as she slept. She'd flipped over onto her stomach, a trick that left him inordinately proud. Why he should be so proud of something every child had to learn to do, he couldn't say. Soon she'd be sitting up by herself, then standing, then walking. Talking. Calling him Daddy.

God, he couldn't wait for that day.

Lauren shifted in her sleep with a quiet murmur and he lay down again, holding her in his arms. Life really was good, he thought as he drifted off to sleep.

And awoke to Lauren screaming.

CHAPTER TWO

LAUREN STEPPED FROM THE BRIGADE'S JET onto the tarmac, glad to be standing on firm earth after being in the air for almost ten hours. The smog-shrouded Washington Monument across the Potomac drew her attention, a calming beacon saluting her return. Would its people be as welcoming?

A sleek, black stretch limo sat with its engine running less than thirty feet away. The driver got out, his windbreaker unbuttoned to allow easy access to the weapon he always wore. After a quick check of the area, he opened the back door, allowing the devil himself to step out.

Cooper Davis straightened his French cuffs and smoothed his perfectly pressed Armani suit before nodding to his driver. Anyone meeting him for the first time might buy his cover as an unassuming businessman, intent only on making a killing on Wall Street; she knew better. He strolled across the pavement with confidence and nonchalance, as if he were about to greet an old lover. Something he'd once suggested. To this day she hadn't decided if it had been a test or a sincere proposition.

She turned her face when he bent down to kiss her so his lips brushed her cheek. One dark eyebrow quirked up at her evasion. "Welcome back, Lauren."

"I'm done, Cooper. I want out." Saying the words both soothed the jumbled thoughts in her brain while setting free the butterflies in her stomach.

"I figured you'd say that." He gestured toward the limo. "Let's sit inside while we discuss your future, shall we?"

She followed him, taking a seat facing him so she could read his facial expressions. As soon as the door closed behind them, sealing them into Cooper's bulletproof, soundproof world, he leaned forward. "There's a problem you should know about before you start planning on retiring."

Problem to Cooper could mean anything from a paperwork snafu to the start of the next world war. From the way every cell in her body went on alert, it was probably more the latter than the former. "I was right, wasn't I? Someone in the Brigade was behind those attacks."

"Yes." He stared out the window, his eyes narrowed. "Frank Harris."

She sucked in her breath. Of all the Brigade's operatives, Harris was both their best marksman and their best tracker. He was also currently the most unstable.

"From what we can gather, he discovered it was you who filed the complaint. He's declared war on you, Lauren."

"I need to leave then. Find a bolt hole. New York. L.A. San Francisco. Somewhere I can get lost in a crowd."

Cooper nodded slowly. "It might work. But it's also possible that Harris will try to get at you through people you care about, Lauren. What'll you do then?"

People she cared about? She'd long been estranged from her only sister and her mother had died a decade ago. Which left… "Chad?"

"It's a distinct possibility."

No. It couldn't be. Hadn't she screwed up Chad's life enough without making him the target of a vengeful ex-CIA operative? "But we're divorced. We've been divorced for almost seven years now."

"Harris was there when you and Thalia had that blow-up a couple months ago. He knows you didn't want the divorce, and he knows you still love Chad. It's possible he'll use Chad as a way to control you or hurt you."

"I never said I love Chad." She'd never admitted it in words but… She thought back, desperate to remember exactly what had been said that day. Was the fight itself enough to tell Harris—and everyone else who'd overheard—how she felt?

"Maybe not in so many words that day, but you did discuss it with Doc Brewer at your last assessment, didn't you?"

"Those files are private." Her eyes widened at his implication. "Harris read them?"

He nodded. "We just discovered someone accessed them last month. We can only assume it was Harris."

"You've read them too," she whispered.

"I'm in charge of the unit, Lauren. I read everyone's reports. But I didn't need a report to tell me you still had strong feelings for Chad." He chuckled darkly. "Luckily for you, the way you insisted on not being stationed back here in the States led everyone else to assume it was out of hatred for Chad, not love."

9

"I didn't want to come back because I wanted to avoid Thalia." Not to mention avoiding the park where she used to take Emily for walks. The hospital where she was born. The Mall where Chad had proposed on the steps of the Lincoln Monument. The condo they had worked so hard to buy that had later become their prison thanks to the media frenzy after Chad had defied Bureau protocol.

"I didn't know what Thalia had done until you two had that fight, Lauren," Cooper said quietly. "If I had, I would have said something sooner."

"Do you know what she did?" She blew out her breath in a slow stream, forcing her shoulders down.

"I know that she was the one who recommended you to Sir Ian when he was running the Brigade and arranged for you to stay out of the country. And I know she hired the solicitor in London so it would look to Chad as if you were seeking the divorce, not him." He tilted his head as he observed her. "Am I right in assuming she's the one who recommended you stay at Tranquil Pastures?"

"Yes. Damn it, I should have flown back here and talked to him face-to-face instead of believing her or that damned lawyer. I had no idea she hated me that much."

"It's not that she hated you, it's that she loves her brother over everything else. And why wouldn't you believe her? What reason would you have had to suspect she was lying when she told you Chad was with someone else, that they were living together?"

Not to mention how he'd never replied to any of the letters she'd sent him that first year or the ones from Dr. Maudsley either. Had Thalia found some way to prevent Chad from getting them? Did it matter anymore?

She closed her eyes in an effort to calm the maelstrom raging inside. At her anger at Thalia for interfering. Her disgust at not discovering the deception for all these years burned with glowing embers of long-simmering resentment. Her rage against Harris burned brightly, its flames licking hungrily at her patience.

"Maybe she wasn't lying. Maybe she just saw the inevitable. We were already in counseling. Neither of us handled Emily's death well. With Chad facing the inquiry and all that press…he was better off without having me distracting him." She settled back in her seat.

She'd mourned the loss of her marriage as much as she'd mourned her daughter.

"So you're not interested in resolving any issues between you and Chad? Seeing if there's still a chance of having a relationship with him?"

God, don't give her hope. It would only be torn from her the way it had been before. She couldn't take losing Chad again. "Just how would we do that after all this time?"

Cooper laid out his plans quickly and succinctly, hope rising in her soul with each step he revealed. The hopes mingled with the thought that he was crazy. Or brilliant. Maybe both. His plan would keep her safe, as well as Chad. Plus, it would let her finally see Chad again, to find out if he hated her for being so weak that she'd walked away when he'd needed her most. No, not walked. She'd run away with her tail tucked between her legs. Cooper was right—she needed to see Chad face-to-face one last time. If for no other reason, to apologize. And explain.

Icy fingers of fear doused the flames. What if Cooper's plan didn't work? He leaned forward. "If you're worried about Thalia interfering again, she's been taken out of the equation. She and Spencer are staying with a friend of mine who can keep them safe until Harris is found."

"What about Sam Watson? How are you going to explain about me considering he doesn't know about the Brigade?" There were so many stumbling blocks to his plan, and Hauberk's owner wasn't the least of them. If he decided not to help, he'd move heaven and hell to keep her and Chad apart. Maybe he'd even known Thalia's plan from the start.

"Ed Weir is on his way to Hauberk as we speak. That's why we're waiting here on the tarmac. If everything goes as planned, you'll be getting back on the plane and flying off to wherever Hauberk plans on stashing you. Somewhere Chad will be your captive audience."

Would it be possible to undo the years of damage that distance and ill feelings had wrought between them? He hadn't answered her question about whether Sam knew about his involvement with the Brigade.

"You'll have that second chance at your marriage you told Brewer you wanted."

Did she dare hope that? Or was it too late? Had too much time built a wall between them? Would it be too high for her to scale, to tear down and rebuild their marriage? Could they stay alive long enough to find out?

CHAPTER THREE

THE LAST INVOICE STAMPED AND INITIALED, Chad placed it on top of the rest in his out box with a sigh. Damned paperwork. It didn't matter how much he signed today, there'd be a whole new pile waiting for him tomorrow.

He opened his top drawer and stared at the silver-framed photograph. Emily with her beautiful, toothless grin, her chubby fist clutching her favorite stuffed bear. Lauren holding Emily, her expression bright and proud. Who knew when that picture had been taken, less than a month later the chuckles and smiles would change to anguished sobs that, to this day haunted his dreams.

The day after he'd been served with the divorce papers, he packed the picture away. The following day he'd retrieved it. He'd compromised by tucking the frame where he could look at it without anyone else knowing. At least he'd managed to wean himself down to looking at it only a couple times a day instead of several times an hour.

"Got a minute?" Hauberk's owner, Sam Watson, filled the doorway. Only the sharpness of his gaze belied the casual way he leaned against the frame. Sam probably knew about the picture and its hiding spot so why the hell did he bother with the deception?

Even so, Chad slid the drawer shut and nodded. "Of course."

Sam closed the door behind him, then settled himself into one of the visitor's chairs opposite Chad, the leather creaking beneath his weight.

They discussed the various reports that had come in the night before, the state of the new office Sam was setting up in Seattle, and a half dozen other unimportant topics that had Chad responding by rote. While Sam droned on, Chad rolled his pen in his fingers. The light fractured on the brushed gold. His sister Thalia had given it to him—crap, fifteen years ago. The day he'd graduated the FBI's academy.

Sam pulled a cigar from his pocket and eyed it. "Damn, I wish I'd never promised Sandy I wouldn't smoke during office hours."

"You're the boss. Tell her it's your office and light up anyway." He suppressed the smile that threatened to break out imagining their assistant's righteous indignation. Sandy would have Sam quivering in a corner in a heartbeat.

As he'd expected, Sam snorted. "Yeah, right. Then she'd move all my files on my computer, or rename them so I couldn't find anything."

"More likely she'd serve you one of those flowery teas she likes. Force you to drink it in front of Jimbo Williams." They both knew how one of their wealthiest and most influential clients judged a man by how he took his coffee.

"Shee-it. I can hear him now." Sam adopted a nasal tone pitched two octaves higher than his usual bass. "No real man puts pansy-assed creamer or sugar in his coffee, Sammy, not if they've got a dick between their legs. Don't send some pinky-wavin' tea drinker to guard me either. You might as well cut off my nuts and call me Sally."

Controlling the smile at Sam's perfect imitation of their client, Chad carefully placed the pen so it lined up with his day planner. "Why are you here, Sam?"

"What do you mean?"

"You didn't come here to discuss Sandy." He lined the day planner up at perfect angles to the blotter that was precisely in line with the desk edge then resettled the pen. "Or the new office in Seattle. Or how the newbie screwed up last night." He looked pointedly at Sam. "By the way, I will talk with him about that, not you."

Sam grimaced and slid the cigar back in his pocket. "Look, the thing is, I got this email linking to an article that's going viral. It's an effort to discredit the FBI not you specifically but they've included that video of you and Lauren."

Shit. "That's old news."

"You and I both know that but we also know the public eats up anything involving a sex scandal. So you're going to be under a lot of scrutiny in the coming days."

"Okay, so I lie low. I sleep in the office if I have to."

"See here's the thing. I think you need to go away for a while. Call that kid—what's his name. Toby? Teddy? You know the one who cuts your grass and collects your —"

"Tommy. Tommy Jenkins."

"That's the one. Have him take care of your place. Book yourself a flight to…" Sam scratched his nose. "…Australia or somewhere. Take yourself a well-earned vacation. You haven't taken a day off since we started. You're due."

15

Australia? Chad blinked before he caught himself. "You think I need to go all the way around the world to distance myself from Hauberk?"

Sam waved him off. "I pulled Australia out of a hat. Rent a cabin somewhere in the Poconos, or, go fishing in Colorado."

"I don't like fishing." But the whole point was Sam didn't want him in DC. What the ever -oving fuck?

Sam's hand drifted to his pocket, seeking the cigar again. With a curse, he lowered his hand, his fingers flexing, restless. "Then head down to Puerto Rico or the Virgin Islands. Sit on the beach with a cold beer. You deserve a vacation."

His balance tilted as if someone had hit him with a sledgehammer. Shit. Sam wanted to distance Hauberk from Chad's sullied reputation. After all he'd done to help build up the company until it was one of the biggest on the eastern seaboard? "You think I'm a detriment to the company. Do you want my resignation? Because if you do, it'll be on your desk in thirty minutes. You want to buy me out too?"

"No, I don't want your resignation or to buy you out. You're half of Hauberk, for fuck's sake."

"But you don't want me around the office. You don't want our clients reminded of why Hauberk got started. Because of my fuck-up."

Sam stood and leaned over the desk, planting his fists on either side of the blotter. "I suggested you get away because you're more than my partner, you're my friend, damn it. I suggested you get away because I hate to see you hounded by those idiots who have a blog and think that makes them a legitimate journalist. I don't want you to have to endure the crap they'll fling at you. You took the heat for me back then, at least let me take some heat for you now."

"I deserved the heat. And those bloggers?" He flung an arm toward the window. "They're right." He played his trump card. "I didn't have to order you to infiltrate the club. We could have found the bastard some other way and Jill would still be alive. Did you ever think about that?"

Sam's expression went blank, and his voice lowered, a sure warning sign he was approaching meltdown. "That's a low blow, even for you. Especially for you."

"But it's true, isn't it? I'm the one who sent you two undercover without authorization. If you hadn't been following my orders, Jill wouldn't have been killed, and you wouldn't have ended up flat on your back in hospital with a bullet a half inch from your heart."

"*Maybe* Jill would still be alive, but Thalia—your own sister, damn it—would be dead. Butchered." Sam folded his arms across his chest, a sure sign he was settling in for a fight he didn't intend to lose. "Who knows how many others Vandeburg would have killed that night? Or gone on to kill another night if I hadn't taken him out?"

Even hearing that man's name was like having someone twist a knife in his guts. Goddamn the bastard. How many people—living and dead—had David Vandeburg destroyed? Was he still destroying?

"It was the MPDC's responsibility to catch him. Not ours." He was relieved that his voice stayed level as he recited the mantra his superiors had chanted right before they'd taken his FBI badge and let the door hit his ass on the way out.

"We both know they were only doing drive-bys. They wouldn't have caught him that way. You think I haven't gone over your decision a million times? Wondered if maybe those headlines were right? You made a decision to catch a serial killer when everyone else turned their backs because of who he was killing. Because of you, we stopped him from killing anyone else."

"The point is I went against orders. I deserve the heat, Sam. Every fucking bit of it." His voice was flat, betraying none of the rage that roiled in his chest. Thalia might not be dead, but she'd never walk again. He'd failed to protect her despite everything he'd done.

"That's not true. And there's nothing you can say that'll ever make me agree with you on that point. I'm not the enemy here, Chad. I'm not worried about Hauberk. I'm worried about you."

"We've been through this before. It'll blow over."

"Yeah, it will. Eventually. But why make yourself a target? Why make yourself miserable trying to avoid people chasing you when you try to drive home when you can get away from here for a while. Away from reporters and bloggers and anyone with a cellphone who are going to hound you, thinking they can get famous if they take your photo."

"They'll be hounding you too."

"Yeah, well, I'm sending Rosie down to her brother's in Puerto Rico, and I can look after myself."

"So can I."

A knock on the door had them both turning around. The head of Hauberk's International group, Troy McPherson, strolled in, looking grim, followed by another man Chad didn't recognize. "Sam, Chad, I'd like you to meet Ed Weir. Ed's got an employee who needs a safe house."

"Nice to meet you, Ed." Sam rose to shake Weir's hand. "Why don't you take a seat and we'll work out the details."

Weir sprawled on the couch instead of taking the leather visitor's chair Sam pushed his way. He hitched one ankle onto his knee. "As McPherson said, I've got a business associate who needs to be kept somewhere safe until we can find the bugger who's threatening her."

Sam hitched his chair around and settled back into it. "Then you've come to the right place."

Chad let Sam run with the company patter while he composed a note to his net wizard Dan to dig up everything he could on Weir. Once the email had been sent, he sat back and assessed their newest client. South African from his accent. Weir's alert gray eyes behind wire-framed glasses assessed his surroundings with the attentiveness Chad expected from his agents. The gaze stopped briefly at the holster beneath Chad's arm before rising to his face.

Interesting and commendable. Many of their clients couldn't have told him what color suit he'd been wearing after talking with them for an hour.

Salt and pepper hair that had once been sandy brown had been clipped so it was no longer than an inch anywhere on his head. There was more gray in the neatly trimmed goatee. Forty perhaps, give or take a couple years. He'd been taller than Troy when they were standing in the doorway which pegged him at six foot two, give or take an inch. A hundred-and-eighty pounds, though that was probably generous.

"I own a few mining ventures back home." Gold or diamonds? Chad wondered. No wedding ring, but a heavy gold link bracelet on his right wrist and a Rolex—one of the Oyster models without diamonds— confirmed Weir had a healthy bank account. Wouldn't a diamond mine owner wear their own product? Gold then perhaps.

"A few months ago, I came to believe we had a mole in the company, someone who might be looking to steal a device we've been working on that should help us find new lodes. So I hired the woman I want you to guard to do some discreet investigation."

"Let me guess—she kicked over some rocks and found a snake?" Sam leaned forward, planting his elbows on his knees.

"Yes. We know who the mole is—and they've been neutralized. Unfortunately the person the informant was selling the information to has taken it personally."

Neutralized? Chad frowned. In his business that meant they'd been killed.

Sam didn't seem as concerned about that line of thought. "You said there have been threats. What type?"

Weir toyed with the hem of his pants on the ankle he'd hitched over his knee. "Someone tossed a Molotov cocktail through her flat's window last Tuesday night. She got out, a little singed but no worse for wear." Chad figured that was an understatement but kept his peace as Weir continued. "My government recommended she return to the States while they investigated the attack. Since I had meetings here this week, I accompanied her."

Troy, who had been leaning against the wall listening silently up to this point, grabbed the remaining vacant chair. "It didn't work though, did it? There's been another attempt. Here in the States."

Weir splayed his fingers over his knees and examined them for a long second before he answered. "Yes. Someone broke into her room and left a tripwire that would have set off a bomb. Lucky for her she's cautious and found it before she set it off."

"Who's your suspect?" Chad cut to the chase.

"The man's name is Frank Harris." Weir pulled out a sheet of paper from his jacket pocket and passed it to Sam, who glanced at it for a moment before handing it to Chad. "According to the investigating officer, Harris has links to a half dozen radical terrorist organizations ranging from Shining Path to Al Qaeda."

All three of them—Sam, Troy and Chad—cursed.

"We can provide a safe location for her to stay—" Sam glanced at Chad, who nodded his agreement, "—complete with armed bodyguards, and a state-of-the-art security system with around the clock coverage. But you're going to have to let us in on the investigation she was running."

"Fair enough." Weir nodded.

Chad left Sam to discuss the monetary details while he considered which safe house to use and who to assign as their principal's guards. He discarded the house in Fredrick as unsuitable. It worked fine for partners seeking distance from a vengeful ex, but with this case, they were talking a more sophisticated threat. The estate in Texas Sam had bought and fitted out the previous year was a possibility, as were the penthouse in New York, the farm just outside Atlanta, or the compound in Vermont. They'd each been set up with a state-of-the-art alarm system, along with a panic room that would be secure even if someone hit it with a hundred pounds of C-4 explosive. For some reason he couldn't name, he ruled out Arlington. New York was out too. It had seen enough terrorism, thanks very much. He checked with the Atlanta office only to discover their safe house was in use. Which left Vermont.

They'd need round-the-clock coverage and someone experienced in dealing with people willing to die to attain their target. He ran through his list of available operatives, weighing each on their merits. The former vice cop Walters? He'd be the best bet as a lead op. The newbie—Campbell—made the list because he hadn't lost that wariness from his hitch in Afghanistan. Wariness was exactly what he wanted, what their client needed. He added and discarded a half-dozen more names. Once he had a plan set in his head, he rejoined the discussion.

Sam leaned back in his chair. "Who are you thinking for lead op?"

Before he could say anything, Troy leaned forward. "Can I recommend Scott Phillips? He's got one of the best strategic minds of anyone at Hauberk."

Phillips? They both knew the operative wasn't one hundred percent recovered from his torture at the hands of the terrorists in Colombia.

"No." Sam's emphatic denial saved Chad from having to denounce Troy's pick. "He can help guard her, but I don't want him as the lead."

"That those people were taken hostage wasn't his fault, Sam, and you know it. There's no possible way he could have known they were being set up," Troy argued, intensity building in his tone. "Plus he'll be extra cautious *because* of what happened down there. Paranoia can be a good weapon sometimes."

Not in Phillips case. Not now. Not yet. "I was thinking Andy Walters."

Sam shook his head. "He's a good man, but I've got a better idea."

He turned his attention back to Weir. "I'm gonna put Mr. Miller himself here in charge of your lady's protection, Mr. Weir. He's former FBI and has learned a few more tricks since we've set up Hauberk."

Damn it. Chad's irritation increased twelvefold when Weir turned a considering eye on him. "From what I understand he's been sitting behind a desk for a while. How do I know he's up to the task?"

Sam hissed in a breath. "Who the hell do you think plans and supervises all our ops? The damned janitor?"

The tension in the air thickened when Weir stiffened, making Chad wonder what his story was, and if he was telling them everything about this threat that they needed to know. Finally he nodded. "All right. So, tell me how you plan to keep her safe."

As Sam had said, who did he think he was dealing with here? An amateur? "With all due respect, Mr. Weir, if I tell you where she's staying, next thing we know there's a leak somewhere down the line—an email that's compromised, a phone conversation that's overheard and passed to the wrong people and your lady is lying on a slab in the morgue beside a handful of our agents. Suffice it to say, we'll keep her in a secure off-the-grid location, surround her with a dozen or more heavily armed agents, and keep her safe until the threat can be neutralized."

"That's where I come in," Troy stated, a darkness in his voice and in his smile.

Weir tapped his index finger on his knee for ten seconds before he nodded. He stood and held out his hand, surprisingly to Chad, not to Sam. "All right, you're hired. But if you fuck this up, Miller, and she gets hurt? I'm coming after you."

"I'll keep her safe." Because who knew if Sam would let him come back. Without Hauberk, without a job to lose himself in, what else did he have left?

CHAPTER FOUR

LAUREN WAS LOST. Neither Ed nor the Hauberk agent whom Ed introduced as Andy Walters would tell her where they were now or where they were heading. Oh, she'd recognized Atlanta's red soil at their first stop, but they'd switched to a ten-seater Lear and from there they'd landed in a series of unrecognizable municipal airports. Each time they'd landed, she'd wondered if Chad would be meeting them there. Each time Ed scratched his beard and shrugged while Andy said nothing at all. She'd given up asking three landings ago when they'd switched from the Lear to a Cessna.

She placed her suitcase at her feet and assessed her surroundings as a white panel van approached. The crisp wind cutting through her thin jacket bore no resemblance to the balmy Georgia weather where they'd first changed planes. No mountains in the distance, no skyscrapers. They could be anywhere in middle America. Or Canada for that matter.

After a simple "stay here", Andy walked across the tarmac toward the van.

Two men jumped out the back, both scanning the area for threats while the driver remained with the van. They'd left their jackets unbuttoned despite the chill in the air, prepared to draw their weapons if challenged. Good. Chad would never have hired wannabe rent-a-cops. These guys were probably ex-police, ex-military. Maybe even a couple of former FBI agents, like Chad. And her.

Andy greeted them then climbed into the van. To warn Chad? She'd never met Walters before, so she couldn't be sure if he knew that she'd formerly been Mrs. Miller or not. If he did know, would he warn Chad and give him an opportunity to back out before they could get him safe?

Moments later Andy reappeared, as did another man. Lauren's heart fluttered into a rapid tattoo then plummeted. It wasn't Chad but Troy McPherson. She barely stifled her huff of disappointment. "What's he doing here? Where's Chad?"

"Watson's probably sending Miller on his own series of hops to make sure he's not followed either,"

Ed guessed. "That way Harris can't simply follow him to find you."

"You're sure Watson bought your cover story?"

"For now. But we both know Hauberk has some fucking impressive contacts within the DSS that even Cooper doesn't have, so they'll find out I'm not who I say I am soon enough. I figure we've got another twelve hours. Maybe more, maybe less."

"We should have come up with a better cover story."

"There wasn't time." He ignored her scowl. "Anyway, once they do figure it out, you and Miller will both be somewhere safe. Who I am won't matter after that. Besides, McPherson knows who you are. If you explain to him about Chad being in danger, he'll help."

He'd help keep *Chad* safe. She wasn't as sure she wouldn't find herself thrown to the wolves.

"While they're not looking…" Ed tucked a strand of her hair behind her ear. To anyone watching, it would appear to be a familiar gesture of a friend, perhaps even a lover. With luck they wouldn't see the transponder he'd tucked into her French braid so she could contact him in an emergency. "It's the only way to keep you both safe, Lauren. Cooper said Harris cracked whatever code they had on the psych files. If he could get in there, who knows if he accessed the rest—you know we can't use any of our own resources."

"I know. There are just so many things that can go wrong. On so many levels."

McPherson said something to one of the men before he and Andy headed their way. His scowl deepened with each step. Troy's gaze flickered between her and Ed, then dropped to her suitcase. His eyes narrowed when he realized she was the only one with luggage.

"You?" He faced Weir. "This is not a good idea."

Ed pulled out his cell phone. "Shall I phone your boss and tell him you're refusing the assignment?"

"So call him. Tell him." His Irish accent was thick today, where last time they'd spoken she'd not heard a trace. Did he affect it for show or did it only slip out when he was upset? "Sam won't agree to this either. Standard procedure is the lead op, or anyone else on the detail for that matter, has no personal involvement with the subject. She's his ex-wife, for Christ's sake."

Ed tucked his cell phone in his pocket, letting Troy get a look at the Sig Sauer under his jacket. He took off his glasses, pulled off his beard. Without the props, the hardness of his personality was reflected in the sharp planes of his face. "You do it our way or…our way. You don't have a choice."

"Yeah. I do. I can put Walters in charge."

"We can't accept that, Troy." Lauren exchanged a look with her partner. They'd worked together long enough that he knew what she intended. After a moment, Weir nodded his agreement. "Whoever is after me may try to get to me through Chad. That's the reason we manipulated things the way we did today. We had to keep Chad safe as well."

"Chad's an effin' target?" Troy tossed in a few more epithets, though they weren't in any language she understood. "Might have been nice if you'd let me in on that beforehand. Or Sam."

"We were afraid you'd tell Miller," Ed admitted.

Lauren jumped in. "If Chad realized he was the target, you know he'd demand to stay in Washington and fight the threat head on. This way we can keep him safer."

"By keeping you both in the same location? Don't you think that's making it a little too easy for Harris? It would be better if you're kept in separate safe houses.   Half a country apart." He was right of course. She'd made the same point to Cooper.

Ed must have realized she was about to relent. He folded his arms and glared at Troy. "You don't do things the way we ask, we'll take Miller into protective custody and hold him where you can't reach him. We can also arrest you for interfering with government agents. That wouldn't look so good for Hauberk now, would it Mr. *McPherson?*"

He'd do it too. Ed would call in the cavalry, who would hustle Troy away and convince him to play ball—by fair means or foul—but if it came down to it, they couldn't press charges. After all, according to the government, the Brigade didn't officially exist.

Maybe it was the way Ed emphasized his name, telling him they knew he wasn't who he claimed that had Troy giving a short nod.

Troy held out his hand to her, palm up. "Give me your bloody cell phone."

Damn it. It wasn't unexpected; she would have made the same demand. She'd just hoped they'd trust her. Good thing Ed had tucked the back-up device into her hair. "I'll need to stay in contact with Ed. Otherwise, how will I know when the assignment's over?"

"Oh, we'll let you use our phones once we've verified everything. In the meantime, I want to make sure you don't text the location of where I'm about to take you to James Bond here. Or that he won't use the GPS chip to track you." No trace remained of the broad Irish accent he'd used earlier. "Then there's the added bonus that it'll bug the shit out of you."

He gestured to one of his companions and tossed the phone to him before turning back to her, his hand outstretched again. "Now your purse, if you don't mind, Ms. *Patrick.*"

She handed it over without a word. Other than her lipstick, and her fake ID there wasn't anything of worth in it. That was a lesson she'd learned long ago.

Instead of him rummaging through it the way she'd expected, he tossed it to the same man who had her phone.

"If this goes wrong, if Chad gets hurt, then I'm taking you out." Aiming his finger as if it were a gun, Troy pointed to them each in turn. "Both of you."

His hand firm on her elbow, Troy marched her to the van where he told her to "assume the position". He did a thorough pat-down, including a sweep with an electronic wand. She held her breath. The Brigade techs had assured them the device didn't transmit any signal while it was turned off. Andy's sweep after they'd met him hadn't picked up the transponder in Ed's pocket, but she wasn't sure if Troy's equipment was the same type or if it was more efficient at sniffing out electronics. To her relief, Troy didn't run the wand over her hair.

Even so she didn't release her breath until he handed the wand back to the other agent and gestured to the van. "Get in."

She climbed in and took a seat on one of the benches lining the side. Troy jumped in and sat across from her, his expression hard. "Lauren Miller—excuse me, Ms. Patrick—" he gestured to the young agent beside him, "—meet Kris Campbell. He and Walters will be part of your primary team." He narrowed his eyes. "I was supposed to leave you here, but I'm thinking I'll stick around a while." The unspoken "To make sure you don't fuck up" hung heavy in the air.

The third man, the one who had taken her cell phone and purse, closed the back door from outside. He tapped it twice and the driver set the van in motion.

"Isn't he coming with us?"

"Nope. He's taking your stuff on a little ride all their own. Just to make sure there's no hidden tracking devices in them." Troy glanced out the side of his eyes at her. "You'll get your purse back whenever the hell this assignment's done."

They drove for several hours before stopping at yet another municipal airport. In the cover of a private hanger, Troy loaded her onto a Sikorsky S-76 helicopter where a second pair of agents waited. One she didn't recognize, though she guessed from his posture he was either a cop or military. The second she did recognize though: Scott Phillips, the single hostage who had managed to escape the guerillas in Colombia before the Brigade had rescued the remainder. Scott gave her a cool look before turning his attention to pulling out a well-worn paperback. She might have thought him engrossed if she hadn't realized he'd turned the page only twice in the next hour.

From the buffeting that had her clutching the armrests, she guessed they were flying over mountains but were they the Guadalupes of Texas, or had they'd flown north and were over the foothills of North Dakota's Black Mountains? Then again, thanks to the nap she'd taken who knows how many hours ago, perhaps they'd doubled back and they were over the Appalachians or even the Laurentians.

At the same time she was thinking of their flight into the terrorists' camp in Colombia, the young agent to her left cursed under his breath about it being Afghanistan all over again. Guess it didn't matter what country or what battle, bad weather and bad flights were universal.

She craned her neck to see out the windows and realized twilight had long since come and gone, and all she could see below them was inky blackness.

Scott peered down at the circle of lights that suddenly blazed beneath them and exhaled. "Thank God."

"Please tell me this is our last stop." She covered her mouth and yawned in an effort to pop the pressure building in her ears from the change in altitude.

"What? Are you bored with our company already?" Troy grabbed a strap over the door when a gust of wind caught the helicopter and it swung around. "You're welcome to leave any time you want. No skin off my nose."

Was Troy still pissed off they hadn't tipped him off to their plans earlier? Or maybe he was offended on Chad's behalf? If that was his reasoning, she had no argument. She stared out the window, watching the stars disappear behind the treetops that whipped around in the downdraft of the helicopter's blades. At least Chad had friends who'd stayed with him this time.

As soon as they'd touched down, the lights shut off, leaving them in the dark. "What's stopping anyone else" —an attacker— "from landing their own helicopter?"

"Oh, I think we'd find a way to discourage any unwanted visitors."

"Let me guess, you've armed your guards with surface-to-air missiles."

A dark smile quirked the ends of his lips but he didn't say anything. Holy hell, how had Hauberk managed to acquire SAMs legally? Just who had Sam Watson fucked to get that type of power?

What was she thinking? He probably obtained them from the same place as the Brigade. Cooper Davis had drawn Sam into his circle without Sam even suspecting what was going on. Or did Sam know about Cooper's real identity?

That single connection between Sam and the Brigade's leader sent another frisson of worry through her. There were too many threads hanging on this case, too many possibilities for Harris to infiltrate Hauberk's network.

A camouflaged guard, complete with infra-red goggles and an MP5 machine gun slung over his shoulder, slid open the helicopter door and glanced around the interior. As soon as he recognized Troy, he touched his hand to his forehead as if he were in the military. "Good evening, sir. Everything's secure."

Troy jumped out first then reached up to help her out, his expression grim. "I hope you bloody well know what you're doing."

So did she.

She ducked her head as she jumped to the ground beside him. Instead of the pavement she expected, soft grass cushioned her landing. Crickets chirped as she took a deep breath, hoping to get some sense of where they were. The scent of fresh mown grass and damp earth filled her lungs. No distant roar of a highway, no bright lights indicative of a nearby city bouncing off the few clouds. With only the stars sparkling above and no moon, she couldn't see much beyond the field they were in. Rolling hills silhouetted the horizon, increasing her suspicion they'd gone in a circle and were now back east. Vermont's Green Mountains? The Appalachians? But where?

Tennessee? Pennsylvania? North Carolina? Did it matter? Not as long as Harris couldn't find them.

Her confidence in their plan faltered when she saw Chad at the far edge of the meadow, four men armed with an assortment of MP5s and M4 carbines flanking him. Even with the distance between them, power emanated from him. His alert posture combined with a quiet confidence radiated his awareness of everything surrounding them. No doubt he'd already evaluated everything either as a threat or for use as a possible defense. Would he head straight for the front gate once he found out she was his principal?

His gaze skimmed over her as they approached, then flicked to assess the two agents at her side. Though his expression was bland, there was no mistaking the tension in his shoulders.

She arrived beside Troy just in time to hear him say, "This wasn't my effin' idea."

Chad looked directly at Lauren but she couldn't read his expression; he'd donned the damned implacable mask he'd learned to use thanks to the FBI and the media. "Noted."

Troy glanced over his shoulder and shook his head. "I think I'll hang around a couple days in case you want someone else to take over."

The agents hung back as Chad stuck his hands in his pockets, something he only did if he was nervous. Which meant his pockets were rarely used. "Hello, Lauren."

I'm sorry, please forgive me for leaving you. For not coming back. I despise your sister for what she did to us. I hate myself for trusting her. I've never stopped loving you. I've missed holding you and being held. I've even missed the way you hog the covers at night. "Hello, Chad."

"Let's go inside." Not cold. Not warm either. Business-like. Detached. Like she was a stranger.

Maybe she was.

As they walked toward the waiting armored van, his palm touched the small of her back, igniting a memory of the first time they'd met at the bar where she'd worked her last year of college. How he'd been so careful with her, so tender and gentle. Oh, he had strength. He'd proven that the way he'd handled the drunken patron who had accosted her. He'd waited around until the end of her shift, his friends having ditched him hours before. Once she was done, he'd escorted her to her car, placing the flat of his hand on her back just the way it was now. The same spark of electricity had zinged through her then too.

Lauren closed her eyes, fighting the guilt welling inside. When she told him what she'd done, when she finally confessed her secret, he'd leave. Worse, he might hate her.

CHAPTER FIVE

CHAD STARED OUT the van's front window in a futile effort to pretend Lauren wasn't sitting mere feet away from him. Did Sam know it was Lauren he'd be protecting?

Damn it, was this all a setup? Some twisted scheme to get them back together? Was Thalia playing one of her manipulative games? Or Sam? No, neither of them liked Lauren. Oh, they'd both liked her well enough until she'd walked away from their marriage. Thalia had been livid on his behalf, while Sam...well, Sam had set him up with an endless number of women. All of whom he'd turned down. Almost all, he corrected himself. He doubted Lauren had been celibate either. The idea of her being with another man turned his stomach. His gaze slid sideways and he checked her left hand. After all these years why should he feel such satisfaction in not finding a ring? He should want her to be happy. Even if it wasn't with him, damn it.

Something about the whole assignment, about the way Weir had come to them and then the way Sam had suggested he get out from behind the desk and take the assignment had the hairs on the back of his neck standing at a ninety-degree angle. Weir had to have known he worked for Hauberk, had to have known he'd once been married to Lauren. So why seek him out? He ran through the meeting and realized that he'd been manipulated—and from the looks of it, Sam had been part of the manipulation. Which made no sense if Sam knew Lauren would be their principal; there was no way in hell he would have put Chad in charge of her protection. Sam, more than anyone, would realize his objectivity would be skewed. It must be obvious from the way he couldn't stop staring at her ankles, remembering them wrapping about him as he positioned himself at her entrance, that he was anything but objective. His cock stiffened at the memory of the heat of her pussy as he slid deep inside her. Shit yeah, his objectivity was completely shot to hell.

When the vehicle stopped in the garage, he got his first good look at her as the interior light came on. There were a few more lines on her face than there had been, no surprise, though fewer than on his. Her hair was longer than it had been last time he'd seen her. Damn it, why was he so turned on by the thought of threading his fingers through her hair, holding her in place while she…Fuck. Fuck. Fuck. *Focus on the mission, not on her sucking your dick, you fucking idiot!*

So much for maintaining any sort of balance. Thank God Troy had said he'd hang around a few days.

Chad led her through the kitchen, introducing her to the couple who took care of the place throughout the year. He'd been here before, for visits and training exercises, so he stood back and watched her. Despite the circles under her eyes, she took the time to greet each of the agents who would be guarding her.

Damn, she looked sexy in that totally oblivious I'm-all-business manner. No one else knew the body hidden beneath that demure white cotton blouse and navy blue slacks. No one else knew the passion and the heat waiting to be released when Lauren let go of her inhibitions. No one else *here* would know, he corrected himself.

As he stood back waiting, he caught Walters slanting him a glance from time to time. Did Andy know Lauren was his ex-wife and now wondered why he hadn't removed himself as lead op? Some great example he was setting to his agents, wasn't he?

Or was Andy attracted to her and wondered if Chad might be jealous if he put a move on her? The little green-eyed monster he thought he'd conquered long ago flared into a dragon that filled the room.

After shooting Andy a narrow glance, Chad grasped Lauren's elbow. "You must be tired. Let me show you your room."

The second he touched her again his whole body reacted as if he'd grabbed a thousand-volt electrical wire—the same sensation he'd had that first night he'd escorted her at the bar. The same way it had each time he'd touched her every day they were married.

"There's an indoor pool, a work-out room, all the comforts of your standard mansion." He'd originally planned to show her them all tonight, but damn it all, he needed distance between them or she'd find herself plastered against the wall, her slacks on the floor at her ankles, her pussy glistening as he buried his cock deep within her.

He pushed open the door to the main bedroom and stood aside, letting her enter first. "I'll show you the rest of the place in the morning."

"No debriefing? Isn't that Hauberk standard operating procedure?"

From the circles beneath her eyes and the heaviness of her lids, she was about to drop. He could have her horizontal in three seconds flat but she wouldn't sleep until he was finished. *Damn it! Focus!* "Sam's got a team working on it. We're safe enough for tonight that we can wait another few hours before we start down that path."

If he had his way, he'd continue the investigation. Until she told him where she'd gone after she'd dropped from his information nets keeping track of her six years ago. Until she told him why she'd done what she'd done years before. Said what she'd said. And not said what he'd needed her to say. *I love you,* like he'd said to her picture a thousand times that first day and the following weeks, followed by *why?*

The pain from coming home that afternoon to discover she'd moved out washed over him. Not in the tidal wave that had once engulfed him. No, time had changed the grief and heartbreak into an acid wash that corroded his honor, his dignity. Having her standing here, so close, captive to his questioning challenged his control.

If he gave into that need, the desire to break her down, he'd never be able to face himself in a mirror again. Those tactics were for the other side.

The bed looming too large in his imagination, he stayed in the middle of the room and let her explore for herself. She opened the closets, frowning as she examined the various track suits, T-shirts and khakis.

Her frown deepened as she fingered a black leather quilted vest. "This is all bullet proof, isn't it?"

"Yes." They'd protect her from close arm fire. Or a sniper. As long as it wasn't a head shot. "For the duration of your stay here, those are the only clothes you'll wear."

"They must have cost Sam a small fortune."

He forced his jaw to unlock. Obviously time hadn't softened her opinion of Sam. "Don't worry about that. Hauberk's doing quite well, in case you haven't heard."

After releasing a slow breath, Lauren nodded. "I wasn't trying to be argumentative. I'm proud of what you've build Hauberk up to be. I'm glad you found somewhere to keep you challenged." Not enough to come back to him. Or even pick up the phone and call him.

She carefully closed the closet door and walked to the window. Probably trying to figure out where she was, he'd wager. In the morning, she may figure out which state they were in. It didn't matter if she knew where they were or not. What mattered was that no one else discovered their location.

"Did you mean what you said to Troy?" she asked after a long moment had passed. "About blaming yourself if anything happened to me?"

"Yes." I worry about everything when it comes to you.

He shut the drape she'd opened, aware he was closing them in completely from prying eyes, aware of the closed door to the hall, how she stood less than a foot away from him, and the massive bed behind her. The subtle fragrance of her perfume tickled his nose. It was the perfume he'd bought her for her birthday the first year they'd been together.

The dark urges, the ones he'd denied for so long, reared up, sending a finger of flame down his spine. His cock hardened, and his balls drew close to his body as his imagination exploded. He wanted to strip her naked and tie her to the bed, leaving her spread eagled and vulnerable. He'd reclaim every inch of her, make a meal of her before spreading her thighs and reminding her who had made her come. Then he'd flip her onto her stomach and take her anally too. And when they were all done, she'd admit she'd never had another lover satisfy her like he could.

What if she had?

Maybe Lauren sensed his thoughts; more likely she'd noticed his burgeoning hard-on, because she stepped away from him. "Are you worried someone might be watching us with a high-powered scope?"

In truth, he wasn't worried about a sniper. She could see how the lights penetrated her linen skirt, how they outlined her trim legs and the V they formed. That the men patrolling the grounds might see her silhouette and have their own fantasies annoyed him no end. "The windows are certified bulletproof, but I'd prefer not to give them a target."

Goddamn it, how many times did they lecture the newbies about maintaining distance and yet here he was, the "I want to fuck you, who cares about anything out there that might put you in danger" poster child.

"Guess that means my five-mile run is off the agenda in the morning?"

His brain dredged up a memory of one of their jogs during their honeymoon. Halfway through their run, Lauren had pointed out a field filled with clover and daisies, bees lazily buzzing from blossom to blossom around them. He'd dragged her into the thigh-high grasses, the thickness of the clover hiding them as he'd undressed her, made love to her. The field echoed with her laughter when he'd plucked a daisy and tickled her with it. Her smile had been brighter than the sun, the sheen of sweat glistening on her skin after he'd rolled off her still made his heart quicken. Finding a field was out of the question, but there was a gazebo overlooking the pond in the valley. If he remembered correctly there was a sofa bed that would cushion them nicely.

Why did he keep imagining them together again? She'd divorced him. Moved out. Moved on.

He stomped the fantasy of them getting back together, even for the night, under his heel. "There's a treadmill in the weight room you can use."

She stopped at the side of the bed, her fingers trailing over the hand-made quilt. She could probably tell him what type it was—the styles all had names like wedding ring or log cabin, but damned if he could tell one from the other. All that mattered to him was that it would keep her warm. Pity no one made the damned things with a layer of Kevlar. Maybe then he'd sleep easier.

"Where are you sleeping?"

Part of him wanted to answer "I'm sleeping in that bed right beside you, just like your husband should," but that part of their marriage had ended even before she'd walked out the door. He shoved his emotions aside. If she wanted a business-like relationship, that's what he'd give her. Tonight. After that the gloves came off.

He stalked to the connecting door and wrenched it open. "I'll be in here. The rest of the team are scattered about the various floors."

Her expression didn't change, her shoulders didn't relax. Did she wish he were sleeping on a different floor? Maybe he should change rooms with Andy or Troy. Distance between them might make this assignment more bearable.

"There are snipers with infrared goggles on the roof, a small platoon of armed guards patrolling the perimeter of the estate, along with a dozen attack dogs protecting the grounds." He kept his voice even, flat. Unemotional. The complete opposite of the needs clawing his guts. "The house has the latest in security— infrared and motion detectors. The doors and windows are wired, and of course you've noticed the cameras in all the main areas. If you want to leave the room tonight, come get me first and I'll give the detail a heads-up that you're on the move." And accompany her anywhere she went.

40

"Afraid I might be mistaken for an intruder?" From the amusement in her voice, she wasn't taking this threat seriously. Damn it. She'd know that despite the precautions they'd taken, there was always a possibility their security could be breached.

"Let me know if you leave the room." He pointed to the button on the side of the night table. "Until we get you set up with a personal panic button, press this to summon the troops if there's any trouble. There's another one in the bathroom, as well as in the closet. Any one of them will set off the alarm and bring the whole team running."

She nodded her head in approval. Her fingers stroked the damned quilt, though he wondered if she was aware of what she was doing.

"Turn this and it'll give you access to your panic room." He turned the center of a rose carved into the mantel. A panel beside the fireplace sprang open revealing a small dark area no bigger than the closet.

She walked closer to examine the tiny room. "Is that a fireman's pole?"

He nodded, unable to stop focusing on how her lips were parted in amusement, soft and plump, glistening with traces of her lip gloss. Kissable.

Focus on the mission, not your goddamned dick. Damn it, she was his principal. She was in danger and needed him focused on her protection.

Why the hell had he let Sam talk him into accepting this assignment? He should leave, let Troy take over the job; he was staying anyway. Except he couldn't walk away. Not now. Not when there was a chance she might finally answer his questions.

He struggled to keep his tone even. "It leads to a room in the basement. It has its own air supply, first aid supplies, encrypted radio to head office, a direct line to the local police, as well as enough food and water for a month."

"Sounds more like a bomb shelter."

"It's that as well. There's a twenty-foot drop straight down, so make sure you've got a good grasp on the pole before you step off. Tomorrow we'll do a practice run."

CHAPTER SIX

HE WAS SO COLD, so controlled. The struggle to keep her disappointment from showing challenged Lauren. Did he not feel anything for her anymore? Did he have none of the desire, none of the need that had tied them together? The desire that had flared inside her, setting her body aglow as soon as she'd seen him? The need for him hadn't lessened over the years. If anything, he was more attractive than he'd been before. She'd always found a man with just a hint of silver at his temples sexy.

How could she get him to stay? To listen to her with an open mind?

She took a step closer. Please don't let him leave. Don't let him close the door between our rooms and shut me out completely.

She'd left the top two buttons of her blouse undone out of habit, but now she toyed with the next one, undoing it, then the next. The fabric parted just enough to show the lace of her chemise. He'd always preferred the fantasy of wondering what was beneath, letting his imagination take over. "Thank you for volunteering to guard me. I was surprised when they said you'd be the lead op."

She *had* been surprised, she realized. She'd been half expecting them to call the whole thing off. Fear that she'd screw things up even more and lose any chance for a reconciliation set in, leaving her frozen deep into her bones.

"I should go." His voice was rough but at least he hadn't moved.

"Please don't." She touched his forearm, letting her fingers rest on him. Heat rose through his cotton shirt, warming her. He was leaner than he'd been. Different. Yet the same. "I don't think I could get to sleep, not after that helicopter ride."

His gaze dropped to her fingers, a frown creasing his forehead. "I'd forgotten you don't like riding in helicopters. Was the flight bad?"

"It could have been better." *You could have been with me.* "There was a bit of turbulence coming over the hills." Or were they mountains? She still hadn't decided. "I haven't had much to eat. Maybe we could find the kitchen, rustle up a sandwich. Talk." About so many things she didn't know where to start. An explanation for why she'd left? For not contacting him? Or even where she'd been and what she'd been doing? Except neither of those were possible thanks to the Brigade's rigid secrecy agreement.

"I'll call the kitchen and ask if they can bring something up for you. As for talking…" He scrubbed his face with his hands, breaking her contact with him. "We can talk tomorrow when we're both fresh." He made touching him impossible by walking to the door and standing inside his room. "When we've both had a chance to sleep on things."

"Stay. I don't want to be alone tonight." Like she'd been for so long.

If she'd had any question he could still love her, the look he gave her removed any doubt. There was no trace of the predator on the hunt he'd had when they were first dating or even five minutes ago, the dominant man determined to win her. This look spoke of the depth of his love and longing. His voice, though controlled, revealed his pain and need even though it was barely above a whisper, husky as if he'd been screaming all night. "I don't think that's a good idea."

"I do." She walked toward him, trying to be quiet, desperate not to give in to the urge to fall at his feet and prove herself to him. If she did, he might react like a wounded animal. One that could turn on her and rip her limb from limb.

No doubts tonight, she told herself, afraid to speak out loud, afraid of breaking whatever force was holding them together. She undid the remaining buttons, tugged her blouse from her slacks and let it drop from her shoulders onto the floor.

His gaze dropped to the lace of her chemise where her nipples had hardened. He'd always loved her breasts, loved touching them, cupping them, kissing them. She debated pulling the chemise over her head, letting him view them unencumbered but decided the peep show might be more provocative. It felt strange to be deliberately leading him on, to have to seduce him. She shimmied out of her slacks and stepped out of them, leaving them in a heap on the floor beside her blouse. Seconds later, her thong rested on top of the pile.

One moment he was clutching the door frame, the next moment she was flattened against it, his thigh between her legs, holding her in place. His voice rasped as he asked, "What's your game, Lauren?" "I'm not playing a game, Chad." *Just doing a lousy job of seducing you.*

He closed his eyes for just a second before meeting her gaze again. "So it's just sex you're looking for? You want to fuck and that's it? Like an itch you want to scratch?"

We cared more about fucking than making sure Emily didn't die, a tiny voice in the back of her head nagged. A voice she thought she'd long since banished. "I miss you. I miss us."

His lips hovered centimeters above hers, his breath warm on her cheek, his eyes locked on her mouth. She expected him to lean down, to take charge, to kiss her. But he didn't. Instead he held himself in check with a rigid control, as if he were fighting a battle. And winning.

"I don't want just one night, Lauren. I want it all back again— us, the way we were. We both know that's not going to happen."

All her doubts crumbled into dust. He wanted her still. "We don't know that."

She tilted her chin and closed the distance between them until her lips brushed his. He didn't move, letting her tongue slide against the seam joining them but not allowing her entry. She wouldn't beg but if he wouldn't accept her kiss, she'd find another way past his defenses.

Her hands flattened over his chest, seeking his shirt buttons. He didn't move as she undid them one by one. His stomach muscles tensed when she parted the opening of his shirt and touched bare skin. She affected him, no matter how hard he tried to hide it. She was so close. If she could just convince him to let go, to give her a chance…she traced the curve of his stomach, up to his pectorals. *Love me. Please.*

As if she'd touched a switch, his body shuddered beneath her fingers. He drew a deep breath, then his lips captured hers, taking command of the kiss. His tongue swept over her lips as if he were sampling her, preparing to feast upon her. He adjusted the angle of his head; his chin rasped over hers, the heat of the razor burn rousing a lingering reminder of their lovemaking long ago.

This was what she'd remembered, what she'd dreamed of all these years. Wanted. Needed.

Yet he hadn't touched her with anything but his mouth. She wanted his hands on her, all over her, every inch of his body touching hers. His chest, his stomach, his hips. More than the hard length of his thigh holding her in place.

Her hands slid around his waist in an attempt to pull him closer but he resisted her attempts. Damn it, if he wouldn't come to her, she'd go to him.

She shifted until they were chest to chest, cradling his erection against her mound, relieved to feel the proof that he wanted her as much as she needed him. The pressure against her chest increased when he captured her wrists, dragged them over her head. *God yes, like that. Take me hard and fast, the way I love.*

Their combined breathing was heavy and harsh in the room as they stood there, panting. Waiting. The hell with waiting. She'd waited too long for this chance, she wasn't going to let it slip away. Holding her breath, she ground her hips against his erection.

With a groan she felt to her toes, Chad dropped his head to her shoulder. His mouth sought out the spot beneath her ear, a spot he'd long ago learned connected straight to her pussy. His teeth nipped the spot, his tongue soothed the sting. Pain followed by pleasure. He repeated it. So hard and fast was out. Slow and easy was nice too.

Without warning, he straightened, releasing her. Instead of backing away, his fingers combed through her hair, one hand cupping the back of her head, holding her in place. "Tell me you don't want this."

"I can't. I *do* want this."

I want to go to bed with you lying beside me, knowing you'll be there in the morning. I want to make you understand why I had to leave, take the pain away that I caused you. I want us.

The way we once were.

Before.

Before the photographers invaded their privacy. Before Emily's death. If it hadn't been for his hold on her, she would have swayed. Instead, she forced the guilt, the grief, back into their cubbyhole and slammed the door she'd created to hold them back.

With a gentle pressure, he pushed her to her knees.

"You know what I want." His voice was rough, as if he'd been shouting in a smoke-filled room all night. Did he realize he only sounded like that when she was in front of him like this? She clung to the knowledge that she still had the power to excite him.

Her fingers shook as she reached for his fly, though with excitement or fear that he'd stop her she wasn't sure.

Could he feel how the blood raced through her veins? Or hear her heart pounding like a bass drum with each inch his zipper lowered? Her breath escaped in a soft puff as she released his erection from its tight confines. She leaned her forehead against his belly, loving the feel of the crisp mat of hair that tickled her nose, the strength of the warm shaft against her cheek. This was where she'd wanted to be for years but never believed she'd experience again. To touch him, to smell him and taste him.

Cupping his behind, she pulled back and nuzzled his cock. Her mouth watering in anticipation, she ran her tongue over the heavy crown. He moaned and his fingers tightened in her hair when she took his whole shaft in her mouth, her lips closing round him adding extra pressure. The globes of his ass tightened as he rocked into her in a slow, steady rhythm. Her body heated at the familiarity of the act. The memories of his taste, his scent, escalated her need for release. She moaned, dropping one hand from his ass to finger her clit.

Whether it was the moan or the loss of contact, he tightened his grip on her hair and pulled her off. "Stop."

He hauled her to her feet, sliding one arm beneath her knee. He kissed her—there was nothing gentle about it. It was hard, demanding. The way she loved. His tongue thrust into her mouth, claiming every inch of her. He broke it off, moving instead to the side of her neck, finding the spot that had her sucking in her breath. She dropped her own mouth to the tender spot where his neck met his shoulder, nipping with her teeth, sucking, leaving her own mark on him, somewhere that would be hidden by his collar. Somewhere no one else would see, but she'd know it was there.

The smooth head of his cock slid between her folds. It brushed over her clit, and withdrew, teasing her until her toes curled against the floor and she couldn't take it anymore. She slipped a hand between them and guided his cock to her entrance.

With a ferocity he'd never shown before, he thrust deep then stayed motionless until his body vibrated with the need to continue. "Do you want this?"

She tilted her hips, closing her eyes at the delicious friction of him filling her. She loved it when he let his aggressive side loose, commanding. Powerful. God, she'd missed this. Missed him. "I want you. I've only ever wanted you, Chad."

His whole body stiffened, the only warning before he withdrew from her. "Bullshit. You divorced me, remember?"

With a cry, she reached out to catch him when he lifted his pants and refastened his fly. He snatched up her shirt and threw it at her. "You even changed your goddamned name back to Patrick as soon as the divorce went through."

She straightened her shoulders. He deserved the truth. "I couldn't stay with you—"

"You were very clear about that. You couldn't be associated with me. What woman wants a man who is more concerned with his sister's life than his wife's career?"

Is that what he thought? Had she really given him that impression? No, more likely Thalia had. "That's not why I left."

"Maybe that wasn't the final straw that drove you out, but it was a big part of it, wasn't it? You never understood why I went against orders, did you?"

"I understood. I still don't agree with your decision to send people in undercover, though I understood why you did it." She deliberately didn't name Sam. "But that's not why I went to England."

"It doesn't matter anymore. Our marriage is over. You got what you wanted. You don't get what you want this time." He released her and opened the door between their rooms. He stopped on the threshold and spoke over his shoulder. "I'll make sure you're protected from this Harris asshole. But once he's neutralized? I don't want to see you again."

Once the door closed behind him, Lauren walked up to it, pressed her forehead against the cool panel and whispered, "I'm not going let you walk away until you've listened to me. Until you believe I left you because I loved you. Not because I didn't."

CHAPTER SEVEN

CHAD RESTED AGAINST THE CLOSED DOOR, stifling an urge to bang his head against it. What the hell had he just done? How had he let it get that far?

I've only ever wanted you. Bull. Shit.

Not after the way she'd had the divorce papers delivered to him. In front of the press by a goddamned process server who looked like he should still be in junior high and hadn't even started shaving yet. The kid was intimidated about serving a guy wearing a gun and had stuttered when he'd asked Chad his name. At least until he spotted the cameras. Then he'd adopted a swagger worthy of a rap star.

At least Sam had his back. Once they had Hauberk up and running, Sam had taken on that damned firm in a long bloody takeover. Hauberk had gained a lot of new customers when they'd finally emerged victorious and that had set them on the path to where they were now—the biggest, most reputable personal protection firm on the east coast.

He stomped into the bathroom and turned on the shower. He undid his shirt buttons, barely stopping himself from ripping the damned shirt off. His still-rampant hard-on caused him some grief with the zipper, but soon his trousers sailed across the bathroom to land in a heap in the corner. Goddamn her.

I'm not playing a game.

Damned straight she was playing a game. With his nuts as the dice.

He stepped into the shower, not caring that the water was too hot. Served him right. He grabbed a bar of soap and lathered his hands. Why the hell had he stopped? Why hadn't he taken his due?

Because he'd be damned if he'd let her drag him back into the hell of thinking she cared for him.

His soapy fist wrapped around his cock, jerking it rapidly. He should have taken his time with her. Tied her to the bed. Teased her to the point of orgasm then left her wanting the way she'd done with him. Or taken her hard, worrying only about pleasing himself.

Fuck. He'd forgotten to use a condom. Who knew who she'd been with? How could he have been so fucking stupid? Because he'd let himself forget they weren't married, forgotten that their rules for sex had changed with the stroke of a judge's pen.

He'd walked on eggshells for too damned long around her. Let her turn away from him when they were in bed for almost a year. Only to come home and find she'd moved out, run all the way to fucking England. He fisted his dick with hard, angry strokes. So he'd made a decision at work without consulting her. That was his fucking job. To make decisions. Didn't she understand he'd had no choice but to send Sam and Jill in undercover? That no one else was stepping up to the plate to protect Thalia? That it was his duty to protect his sister? The same as it was to protect Lauren? The way he'd failed to protect Emily.

With a roar, he slammed his fist into the wall, not caring that the tile cracked. Oh, God, Emily. Even after the coroner's report proved there was nothing they could have done, Lauren had blamed him for Em's death. Hell, how could he blame her? He blamed himself. There had to have been something he could have done but Emily had been cold and rigid even before he'd tried CPR. He slumped against the wall, letting the water cascade over him. Maybe if they had gotten up earlier instead of sleeping in that morning, maybe if…like it had every other time he tried to think of something he could have done, he came up blank. *Enough of this shit*, he finally told himself.

After roughly applying the soap to the rest of his body, he ducked his head under the shower then shut off the water. He grabbed a towel as he considered the question of what he needed to do now.

Phone Sam. Find out if he knew that Lauren would be his principal.

Probably not, he decided. If he had, Sam would have moved heaven and earth to make sure Chad had *not* been assigned as her lead op; Sam didn't like Lauren any more than she liked him.

So Sam had been manipulated too. No easy feat.

He tossed the towel over the shower rail and ensured the edges were aligned before picking up his clothes where he'd dropped them. Once they were properly folded, he strode naked into his room.

Maybe Weir had access to one of Sam's contacts? The one who put the bug in his ear about the upcoming article?

He stopped in the middle of the room. That's where he had to look. Would Sam tell him who had given him the scoop? Once he found out that he'd been manipulated, damned straight he would. Sam would be as pissed as he was right now. Then Sam would ensure that birdie would sing soprano for the rest of his fucking life. He grabbed a shirt out of the closet and replaced the hanger. The routine of dressing, doing up each button one by one helped him focus. His shirt properly buttoned, he grabbed a pair of underwear from the dresser, smoothing the pile he'd disturbed. A clean pair of freshly pressed dress pants were shaken out, and jerked on. Socks. Black. Calf-length so no ankle showed.

By the time he was completely dressed, his movements were smooth, his thoughts focused. Only then did he pick up his cell phone and punch in Sam's number.

No answer.

After leaving a voice message, he booted up his laptop and logged onto Hauberk's VPN. Opened his email program.

"Dear Sam, I respectfully request to be transferred…." No, that wasn't right. "Sam, I need a favor…" Not that either.

He leaned back in his chair and cursed the blinking cursor and what that email represented. Not once had he asked to be taken off a case. Not with the FBI and not with Hauberk. So, damn it, he wasn't taking no for an answer.

A half hour—and numerous deletions—later he finally hit send.

An hour later, he was checking his email for…well, he'd given up counting how many times he'd hit "check mail", when there was a knock at the hallway door. Before he could respond, it opened and Troy walked in.

"Thought you'd like to know the extra men just arrived." Troy closed the door behind him and rested against it. "I've handed out the rotation you drew up. Everything should be good to go."

"Thanks, but I could have handled it."

"I know but I was there checking out the cameras and everything else, so I took care of it." Instead of leaving the way Chad had expected, Troy stayed in place. He tilted his head to one side as he considered

Chad. "You okay, mate?"

Ah. So that was the purpose of visiting in person. Chad nodded. "I admit I was surprised to see her."

His answer didn't satisfy Troy. "Sorry I couldn't give you any more warning than I did, but—"

So he hadn't known it would be Lauren he was escorting either. "It's okay. You were following protocol. You couldn't call me. I understand."

Troy pushed away from the door and wandered into the room. "Helluva a shock for me too when I recognized her."

He'd recognized her? "How did you know her? You've never met her before."

There was a long pause. When Troy responded he didn't look at Chad, and he kept his voice low. "I know about the picture you keep in your desk." He finally looked up. "I wasn't trying to snoop but you were off somewhere—at some meeting with a client or something and we needed a file. Sandy wasn't there so I went through your desk."

Ah. Here he'd been thinking…who knows what he'd been thinking. "Don't worry about it."

There was another pause. "Are you leaving in the morning?" In other words, was Troy to take over?

Would Troy keep Lauren safe? Of course. So why the hesitation in telling Troy he'd already asked to be transferred? "It's under consideration. I tried to get a hold of Sam earlier, but I haven't heard back from him yet."

"Maybe he's trying to smooth things over with Rosie for cancelling their vacation."

Which meant they were probably jumping each other's bones on the desk. Or in that fucking huge shower.

Maybe he was just jealous that Sam's love life had finally come together. Damned stubborn bastard had been closing himself off since Jill's death; it was good to see him finally find someone to love again. Which brought Chad right back around to his original hunch—he'd been set up. Pinching the bridge of his nose, Chad closed his eyes. "Fuck."

He opened his eyes and shot Troy a hard glare. "Is this some way he's come up with to try to force me to get over her? Or get her out of my system or something?"

"Don't know what you're talking about, mate." Troy met his gaze evenly, his voice unaffected. If he'd been anyone else Chad would swear he was telling the truth, but Troy was a consummate liar.

"Why would Weir come to Hauberk if he knew Lauren and I had been married? No one in their right mind would go to an ex-husband to protect a woman." He ran through their conversation again. "No. It's too coincidental."

"And you don't like coincidences." Troy took a deep breath but not once did he break Chad's gaze. "I know you don't believe me right now but swear to God, I had no idea it would be your ex that I'd be escorting." Instead of shutting the fuck up, Troy continued, "You're a better man than me. If it had been my ex, I would have shown her the gate and told her to fend for herself."

He'd considered it. Seriously. Heaven help him if he had to be around her another day. Now he'd had a taste of her, a reminder of what she felt like around him, his dick had taken over his thinking and was seriously planning the various ways he could get her horizontal next time. Not good. "Look, since you're planning on hanging around a couple extra days anyway, why don't I just head back to D.C. now?"

Troy's gaze might have been a laser beam from the look he shot him. "You still fancy her, don't you?"

Fancy her? He'd just jerked off fantasizing about her; that was a big affirmative. "We're divorced."

"That's just a piece of paper, isn't it?" Troy tapped his chest. "But here, inside. That part of you wants another go at her, doesn't it?"

"No."

Annoyed at the line of thought Troy's questions were taking, he stomped into the bathroom and picked up his razor, packing it neatly in its case. When had he decided to leave in the morning whether he'd heard from Sam or not?

"From the looks of your neck, I'd say you may have already had another go at her." Troy had followed him, damn it, and now leaned against the doorframe.

A glance in the mirror revealed Lauren had left a mark on his neck. Damn it, why hadn't he seen that earlier? Because he was too damned busy whacking off. He grabbed the toothpaste and toothbrush and tucked them into their compartment. "Why are you so interested anyway? What the fuck is it to you?"

Troy moved aside when Chad pushed past, trailing him to the bedroom like a goddamned lost puppy. "I may not have been married, but I do know a thing or two about women and how they wind up a man's guts."

Maybe Troy knew about fucking them, but he knew jackshit about keeping them. Then again what did Chad know? He was batting 0 for one right now, wasn't he? "I'm not about to go crawling back on my hands and knees. She was damned clear she didn't want anything to do with me. She thought..." Troy waited a long moment before prompting, "What did she think?" "It doesn't matter."

"It does, though doesn't it? Otherwise you wouldn't have mentioned it."

Unwilling to slog through that emotional swampland, Chad shrugged one shoulder. "She put up with a lot of shit when we were married. Not to mention how the press dragged her through the mud right along with me. Everyone at the bureau thought she'd known what I'd done and had helped cover it up. They made it impossible for her to work there anymore so she ended up having to quit. Even in our personal life—friends she'd had since high school dumped her because of what the press was saying about us."

He'd already lost her by then. She'd pulled away from him after Emily's death. He'd not realized why until that last big fight. By then it had been too late to do anything.

"I'd say they weren't good friends if they walked away when she needed them."

It took Chad a moment to realize what Troy was talking about. "It doesn't matter. Lauren was right. It was my fault the marriage didn't work."

Chad walked to the window and stared out, assessing the guards patrolling the grounds. What were the guards he couldn't see doing? Were they alert to their surroundings? Or were they goofing off, texting their girlfriends or playing some game they'd downloaded on their cell phone?

"Do you really believe that? That it was your fault?"

"I'm the one who fucked up. I'm the reason she ended up with her picture splashed over the fucking tabloids." How they'd managed to get that video of the two of them in their bedroom he still hadn't discovered.

"Bugger that," Troy snarled. "Stop feeling so goddamned sorry for yourself, man. From what I've heard, there was nothing you could have done to have saved your daughter's life. People die and most times there's nothing you can do about it but suck it up and move on."

Chad whirled to face him. "You're preaching to the choir about death. I know all about it. My father was killed in the line of duty— shot by a goddamned drug addict during a routine traffic stop. My mother was murdered eight years later." He clenched his fists "Less than a year after Emily died, my sister got shot. She may not be dead but she's in a wheelchair because I couldn't protect her. So do not talk to me about how *people die.*"

"Take your head out of your goddamned arse for once and stop blaming yourself. You were, what, eleven when your father was killed? There is no way you can blame yourself for that. You were living in Boston when that sick bastard lured your mother into showing him that home she had up for sale. There was nothing you could have done to have helped. There was nothing anyone could have done. As for your daughter, her death wasn't your fault either. It is what it is. Stop blaming yourself."

It is what it is. How he hated that phrase. Nothing was as it should be. The anger, the ire, drained from Chad as if Troy had pulled a plug, leaving him with an emptiness that was even worse. "I keep thinking I should have seen something, some sign."

Troy squeezed his shoulder. "Lauren feels the same way. Not about you being responsible, but that she should have seen something too. You two need to talk before you leave, about that if nothing else."

"How would you know?"

"I just do."

They'd been stuck on a plane together for hours with nothing to do. If Troy had recognized her, maybe they'd talked. He closed the cover on his suitcase and zipped it shut. *Stay. I don't want to be alone tonight.*

What about tomorrow night? Or last night? Or the night before? She'd been the one to run away last time, now he was walking away from her. Self-preservation, instinct, he didn't know which was placing the suitcase by the door, but he'd be damned if he'd let her rip his heart from his chest again.

Maybe that was the question he should be asking himself: why did she still have the power to hurt him after all these years?

"Because you still love her. More's the pity."

He stared at Troy. "What?"

"You asked how she still had the power to hurt you." He'd said that out loud?

"I know you look at that picture in your desk a half dozen times a day. You still love her." Troy tapped the top of Chad's suitcase. "So, what are you going to do about it? You going to run? Because that hasn't worked for either of you so far, has it?"

CHAPTER EIGHT

FROM THE BRIGHTNESS OF THE CLOUDS overhead, the sun was up on the other side of the mountains, though it had yet to reach the lower edges of the hill. A thick mat of pine needles and already-fallen leaves littered the path, crunching beneath her feet as Lauren jogged along the path. She ducked beneath an overhanging branch, taking care to make sure it didn't fling back into her companion's face.

She'd hoped to slip out of her room that morning without anyone noticing. But as soon as her door had opened, Andy had stepped out. The lack of time between his door opening and hers made her wonder if he'd been listening for her. Then she noticed the camera mounted on the wall opposite her door. Not listening. Watching.

She glanced back to assess him. Like her, he'd dressed for the occasion, although his holster held a Glock whereas hers had a Sig Sauer. Something about the way he carried himself told her he'd not be afraid to use it. An intricate full-arm tattoo flowered from beneath his tee's sleeve, stopping just above the wrist. Probably so it wouldn't show beneath a dress shirt. "How far do you normally run?"

Andy ducked beneath a tree branch before he answered, "About five K. I run more on the weekends."

They'd run the perimeter of the compound—or the estate, as Chad referred to it—twice, which meant they were approaching the length of a regular run for them both. Although there was a slight sheen of sweat on his forehead, Andy wasn't breathing hard yet, which gave her the impression "more" probably meant he ran marathons. What impressed her most was that they weren't running on a smooth city sidewalk. The rough trail they followed wound its way up and down the side of the...well, it was more than a hill but less than a mountain. They were high enough that the air was thinner than in D.C. Not as thin as in Colombia, but Andy wasn't showing any signs of having trouble getting enough oxygen.

Face it, she told herself, *the man was in shape.* Chad had chosen his people well.

Pounding on the track behind them had her turning and ducking behind the nearest tree. Her hand was still reaching for her holster when she realized Andy already had his gun drawn and his body placed between her and whoever was intent upon catching them. Two seconds later, Troy jogged into sight and Andy lowered his weapon. "Hey, boss, what's up?"

Troy hardly looked at his man as he spoke, his focus completely on Lauren. "I'll take over here. Why don't you get some grub?"

His gun holstered, Andy nodded and sprinted off toward the main house.

Lauren stepped back onto the path, watching him disappear down the hill. "He's good."

"He is. Damned good. But I wasn't the one who hired him initially. That was all your ex-husband's doing." With the emphasis on ex. "Thought you should know—Chad's asked to be reassigned."

Shit. "You can't let him leave. Not if you want him to stay alive."

His hand slapped arrhythmically against his thigh as he stared off in the distance, no doubt considering the same ramifications and alternatives they'd already gone over. "How long do you think you're going to be able to fool him?"

"Hopefully until we catch Harris."

He turned a bland look on her. "That's not what I was referring to."

This was not a conversation she wanted to have. With a sigh, and a silent prayer that Troy wouldn't follow, Lauren reversed her course.

"Running won't help. I want an answer and I want it now."

"I'll answer your question once we're farther away. I don't want Chad overhearing this conversation." She pushed on, speeding up if he got too close. The muscles in Lauren's legs ached, protesting each step she took as the path led back up the side of the hill.

"You're not going to lose me if that's what you're hoping," he said finally, not even breathing heavily, goddamn him. "Now tell me, when are you going to tell him the truth?"

"After we neutralize the threat." Then she'd lock them both in her room until he agreed to give their marriage another chance. Or he'd convinced her there was no way she deserved one. Which was more likely.

He slapped at the branch she'd pushed out of her way but threatened to hit him. "Why don't you just tell him the truth? It's his life—he should get a choice in how it plays out."

"So why didn't you say something to him in the office when the arrangements were being made? You could have told him last night too, but you didn't." If he had, Chad wouldn't be sleeping at the desk in his bedroom the way he had been when she'd checked on him.

Troy cursed again. "Let's get this straight; I'm not doing this for you. I'm doing it for him. Poor bugger's been through enough without Cooper and you playing mind games on him. He's had enough of that, don't you think?"

She'd had enough mind games to last her a lifetime. Thalia's. Cooper's. Was that what she was doing to Chad? Manipulating him? No. Other than keeping him safe, once Harris was found, she'd accept whatever decision he made. For better or worse. She ducked under an overhanging branch. "It's not a game."

He grabbed her and forced her to face him. "You know what I don't get? You work for an organization that's sanctioned both by the feds and the U.N. for all you try to claim it's not associated with any of them. Which means you probably have a safe house or two of your own hidden away. Why not just grab Chad and protect him yourselves?"

"That's not our style."

"Bullshit." His gaze hardened. "You've been infiltrated, haven't you? Harris is one of your guys, isn't he?"

She turned her back on Troy and started running again. If he wanted to continue the conversation, he'd have to follow her. Which the bastard did, damn it.

"What? Didn't like being questioned? Fine, you'll have to answer Chad's questions later."

"I know." God help her then.

"Here's another question for you: why did you do this? Arrange to be placed in the same facility as him? Weir's story could have served its purpose—we could have guarded you separate from him.

But you guys manipulated us just so you two would be put together. Why is that?" "It's none of your business."

"Yeah, lady, it is. Miller is my friend and I don't like people who playing fucking mind games with my friends."

"Guess what, you don't know everything about me. Or Chad. Or our marriage."

"I know more than you think."

"You know nothing but what you overheard when I was talking with Thalia." Half the building had heard that argument.

"I know you ran away after accusing him publicly of having been responsible for the death of your daughter."

She stumbled and had to grab onto a sapling to steady herself. "You don't know what you're talking about. You weren't there."

"No, I wasn't there but I know what you left behind. Chad's a man with more dignity and honor than most men have these days. A man who was only trying to protect his family the best way he knew how, and you walked away from him when he needed you."

"I was there for him while the press camped on our front lawn, taking pictures through the cracks in the blinds that got plastered over the internet for anyone and their brother to see. I lived with the headlines speculating if we were into sex games like those from Thalia's club. Do you have any idea what it's like to be the butt of night show monologue jokes when a video of you and your husband having sex goes viral?"

She still hadn't figured out how they'd filmed that footage. "I lived with the neighbors who gave us sideways glances every time we left our front door, with those who didn't bother with glances but with outright suggestions of what they wanted me to do for them. You weren't there when I discovered my coworkers were passing around Photoshopped pictures of me or hear the snickers and suggestions when I walked past them."

She whirled away from him and stared at the trees swaying overhead. Her body quivered, torn between wanting to race along the path, to put as much space between her and Troy as she could, and decking the smug bastard. "You weren't there when the press followed us to the cemetery to visit Emily's grave on her first birthday." What should have been her first birthday.

"Do you know how it felt to have to watch the news showing your daughter's gravesite being trampled by press who didn't give a damn about respect? To find graffiti and damage done to her gravestone the next day?" She forced herself to face him again. "I had to deal with the catcalls and hate mail. I was there for the death threats. And the bomb threats. Me. Not you. So don't you dare judge me."

"No, I wasn't there." His voice was soft, almost gentle, but the intensity in his gaze, his whiteknuckled fists, told her he was barely hanging on to his own temper. "But Chad was. And you let him think it was all his fault when it wasn't."

"I didn't." She closed her eyes and swayed. She had. Which was one of the reasons she was here, wasn't it?

"I know what you told him, Lauren. I also know what really happened."

"No, you don't. You don't have a fucking clue." Only her therapist knew what really happened. And Cooper. And Harris if he'd gotten into her psych files. So much for doctor/patient confidentiality.

Troy clamped his hands on her shoulders, ensuring her attention. "All Hauberk employees have to have regular psychiatric evaluations. Even the managers. Chad thinks you hold him responsible for not being able to save your daughter. Apart from his decision to protect his sister, he thinks that's why you ran from him."

She resisted the urge to press her fingers to her mouth in horror. Did Chad truly believe she thought him responsible? "He did everything he could. I don't blame him."

Troy stared down at her like a judge and jury ready to pronounce sentence. "I've read your reports too."

"No. You couldn't have. Those are sealed and kept in…" Dear God, had it been Troy who had broken into the Dr. Brewer's files? Not Harris?

"You think you're the reason Emily's dead." His voice dropped to a whisper. "That if you'd just said something about what you'd been worrying about, if you'd talked to your doctor or her pediatrician you could have saved her. You think you knew there was something wrong with her, didn't you?"

"No!" Except Troy echoed what she'd wondered all this time so her denial lacked conviction. Why else had she been so obsessive about checking on Em all those months?

Grief knifed through her as sharply as it had when she'd cradled her daughter's lifeless body in her arms. If it hadn't been for Troy's hold on her, she'd have dropped to her knees.

Damn it. She'd locked that guilt away deep inside, hadn't had to face it in years. Damn him for releasing that flood gate. Needing to strike out at everything that had happened in those years—the press, Thalia's manipulations, even Chad's failure to come after her, to leave the States and fly to England, had her struggling to breathe. She flattened her hands on his chest and pushed—hard—making him stumble back. "Fuck you. You haven't a clue what you're talking about."

"Chad is still hurting. Same as you. When neither of you could have saved your daughter."

"I know that!"

"Then for Christ's sake, stop playing your stupid fucking games. Stop hiding from him. Tell Chad the truth and let him up his own mind about everything. About you. And about why you made those decisions. And where you went after you left him."

CHAPTER NINE

"WE'RE POSITIVE, CHAD." Sam stared out from the video chat session on Chad's laptop screen. "There's absolutely no record of an Edward Weir owning any mines in South Africa. There's no record of him coming into the country any time in the past year either. I've put out some feelers about this Light Brigade Investigators' firm Weir says he hired. They're legit as far as we can tell, and the guy I spoke to at their international office told me exactly the same story as Weir."

Chad leaned back in his chair. If this had been a setup Sam wouldn't have told him Weir hadn't checked out. He'd be telling him the threat had ramped up or something to keep him there. "I'll ask Lauren about it. She may be able to shed some light on the situation."

"Nah, tell Troy to do that. He can be in charge until we figure the rest of this shit out." Sam rolled an unlit cigar between his fingers and frowned. "I'm telling you, buddy, something's hinky about this whole set-up. I look back on it now—the email about the story on you, then Weir coming in right after?

I'm thinking they were deliberately timed that way but damned if I can figure out why."

"But why? What would Weir have to gain?" Why would Lauren lie to him? No, this had to be a setup; he just couldn't figure out their aim.

"Hey, bud?" Sam interrupted. "I hate to ask this, but is it possible Lauren's a spy for another protection agency? That maybe she's workin' for our competition and they're lookin' for a way to discredit us? Or at least discover our weaknesses?"

"If I were the competition, I wouldn't use the ex-wife of an employee. That would make them more suspicious." He'd set it up with someone they didn't know. Someone who they wouldn't suspect to be anything other than who he'd said they were, and he damned well would have made sure their cover story was in place.

Sam cursed softly. "Listen, buddy, I don't like this. I feel like a goddamned puppet being manipulated and I don't that feelin'. Why don't you head back? I'll have Sandy arrange a flight for you out of Burlington."

Puppet being manipulated. If Sam hadn't agreed to let him leave, he would have tagged Sam as the prime puppet master. So just who was pulling the strings? And why?

Chad straightened the laptop so it was aligned with the edge of the desk. "Tell Sandy I should be able to make it to Burlington by this afternoon. I still have to find Troy and tell him I'm leaving."

Sam leaned forward, his face taking up nearly the entire tiny video chat screen. "You watch your back while you're there, buddy, you hear? Tell Troy to watch his too."

"Thanks. I will." Yeah, Sam wasn't behind this. Sam would have just locked him in a room at his private club. "You know for a while there I thought maybe you and Thalia were setting me up."

"Shee-it, no." The cigar disappeared, jammed back into Sam's pocket with such force Chad was surprised the seams hadn't ripped. "No, if I wanted to do that, I would have locked you up in a room at the club until you listened to me."

Chad suppressed his smile. Did he know Sam or what?

"I would have staged a fuckin' intervention or whatever the fuck they're called," Sam continued. "I fuckin' well wouldn't have locked you in with the ice queen and hope a little global warming set in."

"You used to like her. She's the one who…" Encouraged Sam to date Jill. Ah. Strange how time and distance sometimes made things so much clearer. "She and Jill had been good friends, Sam. She was upset when she said what she did. Losing Jill right after…"— Emily— "She was confused. Upset."

"She was a self-centered bitch." A feminine gasp from off-screen told him Rosie was listening.

He lined up the pen with the mouse pad. "She needed me and I wasn't there for her. Not really. You were…collateral damage."

"She wasn't there when you needed her either, damn it. You need to get your head out of your ass and see she's not good for you. Sure, she was a good fuck, but there are lots of women who would do you in a heartbeat."

"Sam!" Rosie appeared on the screen. She hooked an arm around Sam's neck and settled in his lap. The sappy look on Sam's face should have been amusing, instead, he was jealous. "Chad, do you still love her?"

Behind her, Sam snorted and shook his head in disgust. "You see him dating anyone else lately, Rosebud? Nearly eight fuckin' years he's gone on a handful of dates with women I've set him up with. I doubt he's gone through a box of condoms that whole fuckin' time."

Rosie placed a finger over Sam's lips and ssshed him before facing the webcam again. "Chad? You need to get things straight with her. Talk to her. Listen to her." She flattened her fingers over her heart. "Listen to what your heart is telling you. Because it sounds like you still care for her."

Behind her, Sam rolled his eyes. "Yeah, fuck her and get her out of your system. Then dump her on her ass out the front gates."

That pearl of wisdom earned Sam a slap on his hand. Damn, Sam was lucky to have convinced Rosie to come back to D.C., to agree to date him again. Just how much groveling Sam had done in New York, neither of them would say.

That's how things should have happened with him and Lauren, yet it hadn't. Which was his own damned fault. Lauren had probably expected him to fly after her and beg her to come back, the way Sam had flown after Rosie. Instead he'd let Lauren go.

"Thanks Sam. I'll phone you when I get back into D.C." Chad clicked the mouse on the "end chat" button and the chat session disappeared from the screen.

The conversation replayed in his mind as he closed up his computer. *Fuck her and get her out of your system.* Didn't Sam realize Lauren was his drug of choice? That if he fucked her again, the way he'd came too damned close to doing last night, he'd never get her out of his system?

Talk to her, Rosie had said. *Listen to her.* Right. Well, Lauren sure had some talking to do. About who Weir was and who she worked for. He just had to decide whether she'd be talking to him or to Troy for that conversation.

A quick check of her room showed Lauren hadn't returned. The closed circuit cameras revealed her location—she'd gone jogging and was a third the way out to the far end of the property. He could wait until she passed by the house and catch her then.

Ah, hell, he needed to jog this morning anyway. He lost seven minutes dashing back up to his room and changing into his sweats. By the time he met Troy halfway out, he'd warmed up nicely. Both his muscles and his irritation.

Troy slowed as he approached Chad. "If you're looking for Lauren, she's up the hill."

Once again he debated turning around and waiting for her to return to the house but decided against it. If it ended up with her screaming at him, he'd rather do it where no one could hear. He found her pounding hell bent for leather down the path.

"Lauren."

She glanced over her shoulder but kept running. "Leave me alone right now, Chad. I'm not very good company."

His step hesitated as he almost did turn around. No, if someone was trying to discredit Hauberk through her, he owed it to Sam—and Troy—to find out just what the hell was going on. "Lauren, slow down, damn it."

She didn't.

He sprinted, thinking he was fresher and could take advantage of her exhaustion. Considering she'd probably run close to five kilometers already, it still took a concerted effort to catch up. "You're worn out and if you keep this up, you're going to trip over a root and twist your ankle." Not to mention he needed to talk to her face-to-face instead of to her ass, as nice a view as that was.

With a huff of exasperation, most likely more at herself than at him, Lauren slowed down and a few hundred yards up stopped entirely. Breathing hard, she braced her hands on her knees.

"Just leave me alone for a while. Please."

"That's not what you were begging me to do last night. Or have you forgotten how you got on your knees and sucked my dick?" *Fuck. That was a stupid—*

73

Before he could finish the thought, Lauren did a neat sweep with her foot he wasn't expecting and he found himself flat on his back, the breath driven from him. He rolled to a stand and watched her disappear down the trail.

So she wanted to play it that way, did she? Game on.

They ran half the trail dodging and evading each other's attacks. At some point, he couldn't figure out when, his anger morphed to arousal. He found himself admiring that she'd run more than twice as far as he had yet showed no signs of tiring; he also found himself admiring the swing of her hips as she ran in front of him, the bounce of her breasts when they wrestled. Until they reached the steep hill and she stumbled over a protruding root as he'd predicted would happen. Launching himself at her, Chad trapped her by using his full weight on top of her.

She fought him for a moment, attempting to buck him off, then relaxed. Chuckling, she reached up and skimmed a finger down his jaw. "You still get turned on by the chase, don't you?" Considering the erection jabbing into her belly he could hardly deny it.

"Never could understand guys who liked submissive women." He ground his cock against her mound then, with a sigh, sat back on his heels but stayed straddling her. "You realize my guys are probably watching on the monitors."

"They even have cameras out here?"

He tipped his head toward the gazebo further down the path. "There are a couple mounted down there. They're motion activated and we're within range."

"Shit." She shoved him off and scrambled to her feet. "What did you want that you had to chase me for this far?"

He opened his mouth to say "I'm leaving" but the words wouldn't come. The sensual side she'd shown him yesterday, the *I want you. I've only ever wanted you* hunger in her eyes had returned.

"Yesterday you said we needed to talk. I told you we'd talk this morning." Talk? He wanted to bend her over the trunk of that fallen tree and fuck her from behind. He took a deep breath and centered himself. "I told you not to leave your room without me, or are you incapable of following orders?"

She straightened, holding her chin high. "I brought my gun and one of your guards. It was only a matter of time before I returned." Her eyes narrowed. "Besides, Hauberk guaranteed this as a safe house and their employees as well-trained professionals. Are you telling me this place isn't secure?"

"We can't—oh, for Christ's sakes, just come with me." Chad stalked down the path toward the pond, wondering if she would indeed follow him. He made it almost to the gazebo before he chanced a glance back and realize she still stood there, her shoulders slumped. "Don't play any more games with me, Lauren."

"I wasn't playing a—" Her voice fractured and she cleared her throat. If it were anyone else, he'd think she was fighting tears, but her eyes were dry.

"You were sleeping when I checked on you this morning," she continued, her voice firm once again. "I know you were up late last night so I didn't want to disturb you." When he didn't say anything, she explained, "I saw the light under your door, that's how I know you were up until at least four this morning."

Which meant she'd been awake too. Plotting a sob story? No, that wasn't Lauren's style. There were circles beneath her eyes he realized as he took a closer look, lending her an air of fragility that belied her defiance. He reminded himself all wasn't what it appeared. "I've got some questions for you."

She opened her mouth as if to snap something in return but instead she simply sighed. "Fine."

Fine. Now there was a landmine of a word.

His hand firm on her elbow, he followed her up the wooden steps leading to the gazebo overlooking the pond and the rest of the valley. He steered her to the canopied sofa where she sank onto the cushions with a soul deep sigh.

She'd run hard, worked up a sweat so her T-shirt clung to her curves, making him acutely aware of the hard nipples jutting from the fabric. Except for the Sig Sauer in its holster, she was the ultimate picture of femininity and composure, her feet neatly crossed at the ankles, her hands clasped on her lap.

Concentrate on the mission, damn it.

Instead of folding his arms the way he wanted to, he let them hang loose and leaned against the center post in an attempt to appear relaxed. "I want to talk about why you're here."

"Okay."

"You work for a private firm called Light Brigade Investigations, Inc."

Her gaze met his for just a second before it flitted away to focus on something on the other side of the pond. "Yes."

"They sent you to South Africa to determine if a mole in Edward Weir's mining company was selling corporate secrets."

"Yes." If he hadn't been watching her carefully, he may not have noticed her fingernails dig into the skin of her knuckles. Or the almost imperceptible tightening of her shoulders.

She'd just lied. Why?

"And you uncovered someone who led you to a man named Frank Harris."

"Yes."

Chad swore under his breath. "If you keep giving me one word answers, we'll be here all frickin' day. Don't you want us to catch whoever it is who has forced you to hide?"

"Of course I do."

"Then tell me why you're really here."

He continued questioning until he'd verified her story corroborated with Weir's. Which of course it did, damn it. The silence between them hung heavy, as if someone had hung a blanket between them. It wasn't that he didn't have questions for her. The big one, the *Why are you lying?* one got shoved aside by the others crowding his mind. *Where have you been? Why didn't you call me, tell me where you were going when you moved from London? Or Paris?*

A damned email might have been nice. A text message. Something. Anything to let me know you were all right.

Did you know I still dream about you? About us?

He heaved in a breath and found himself staring at a spot across the lake, absently wondering if they were staring at the same tree. Damn it, this was the reason why ex-husbands should never be assigned to guard their ex-wives.

Focus on your mission. Which was…what? Was she in danger? Or was this some sort of setup to discredit Hauberk?

He lost track of the time they'd been there when she suddenly spoke, startling him. "I suppose you guessed I haven't been living in London for a while now."

"Yes." Any of his attempts to contact her had gone unanswered so he'd used his Hauberk resources to track her. "You ran the security for a fancy spa, Tranquil Pastures, for six months in Kent, then quit and moved to Brussels. Six months after that you moved to Paris where you were hired to guard the wife and children of a Saudi Arabian family."

Her gaze darted back to him before returning to the pond. "You've got good sources."

Not good enough. From there, she'd dropped from his radar. "And now you work out of your company's offices in Rome."

"Yes."

He shoved his hands in his pockets and walked to the stop of the stairs, blocking the exit. "Did you know there's no record of an Edward Weir owning any mine, diamond, gold or otherwise, in South Africa? Or anywhere in Africa, Australia, Canada or the States?"

"He's not the only owner, so the mine isn't in his name. It's registered to a numbered off-shore corporation." She finally looked at him, her mask of composure firmly in place.

"Did you also know that there's no record of him coming into the country in the past six months? Oh, there were several Edward Weirs but none fitting your boss's description."

Once again that spot across the pond got her undivided attention. "Maybe you aren't looking in the right places."

Why was every nerve ending twitching? Oh, yeah, because she was *lying*.

"I've spoken with Sam, Lauren. Yesterday morning he got an email linking him to an article trying to discredit the FBI on the net that's going viral. Featuring all the failures the FBI have had. Sort of a 'where are they now and how did they change American history' type story. Guess who's front and center?"

"I'm sorry."

He bit back his "Too little too late, sweetheart," instead continuing with, "Ten minutes later Weir appeared at the office. Told us about you needing protection. Laid out what he needed. Not once did he mention you by name. But he knew we'd been married, didn't he?"

"Yes." He could hardly hear her whisper above the wind in the trees.

"You know it's never SOP to assign an ex-spouse as a bodyguard. There's too much baggage attached." The truckloads they had between them could fill Chesapeake Bay. "So, what's the story?

Is there someone after you? Or is this some elaborate scheme to discredit Hauberk?"

"There really is a threat." This time she looked at him, her hands were still together in her lap, but her fingernails no longer scored the skin. Her expression was composed if rather sad, not tense. Her shoulders slumped, and a hint of vulnerability pierced her armor. "LBI caters to very rich clients who need discreet investigations—blackmail, that type of thing. I'd investigated this scumbag who was blackmailing a certain high profile movie star. Part of the fallout of it was the scumbag's wife divorced him. I had taken some incriminating pictures of him as part of my investigation and so I was called to testify against him at his wife's petition for full custody. Which she got based mainly on my testimony. Next thing we knew he'd hired Harris."

When he'd first met her, she'd been quick with a retort, her eyes sparkling, her mouth pulling up at the ends in the most provocative grin he'd ever seen. They'd laughed at lot in those early years. Before. Even in their more serious moments, they were in tune—finishing each other's sentences, knowing when the other needed a touch, gentle or not, to ground them. For a while there, things had been so good between them he'd have taken a bet that their marriage could have survived anything.

What he'd give to see her smile. Just once. The way she had…before. The memory of finding her on her knees, sobbing, clutching Emily's lifeless body. Of the tears streaming down her face at the funeral. Tears that dried up and never reappeared. She'd held herself in ruthless control after that. She'd closed herself off from him and everyone.

He shook his head and forced himself to focus on his objective. Damn it, why the hell was he still so attracted to her? *Concentrate on the mission. Stop letting her distract you.* This was the very reason he shouldn't have been put in charge of the op. "So, who's Weir?"

"Ed's my partner. Or, he was my partner. I've told my boss that once this is settled, I'm quitting."

"Why come to Hauberk? Couldn't your own people protect you?"

"LBI's a small company. We don't have the type of safe houses Hauberk does, or the manpower to protect me. Harris is…dangerous."

She believed the bit about the danger, but there was something else going on with her. But what? "So you manipulated Sam and me until I was assigned as your lead op."

She nodded.

"So there's no online story? Or there is because someone in your firm put it up. Then they emailed Sam to convince him to assign me to your case."

"There really is a story, but no, we didn't publish it. As for the email? I don't know if one of my people sent it to him or not."

Shit. Someone in her firm must have. The timing was too coincidental. And he didn't believe in coincidences. He grabbed the pine railing and stared over the lake. "Why me, Lauren? Why seek me out after all these years?"

"Because you're not the type of man to walk away from an assignment. Because I trust you."

He dismissed that as flattery. Or prevarication. She hadn't trusted him all those years before. From the location of her voice, she'd moved. Was coming closer.

His shoulders stiffened as if he were expecting her to plunge yet another metaphorical knife between them. "You didn't trust me when we were married. Why in hell would you trust me now?"

The footsteps stopped. "I trusted you! I've always trusted you."

He snorted. "You trusted me not to follow you to England."

She'd been right. He'd let her walk away. Until yesterday he'd questioned that decision every day. Now, with her here, he wasn't sure that perhaps it hadn't been the best decision he'd ever made. The ability to live with the hole she'd left had been torn from him and when this was over, he'd have to rebuild everything all over again.

"I didn't leave you because I didn't trust you. I left because I trusted the wrong person's advice. I made a bad decision, Chad. Haven't you ever made a decision you regretted later?"

Instead of feeling the satisfaction, the relief he'd expected, anger surged inside him, a low burn that boiled over. "It's taken you eight years—eight fucking years—to find me to tell me that? You threw everything we had together away, Lauren. I gave you my word that I would be there for you. I stood up in front of a judge and promised to love, honor and cherish you, no matter what. So did you."

"I know. I should have stayed." Her quiet answer slipped into his brain, into his heart, a soothing balm tipped with barbs. "I was mixed up; I wasn't thinking clearly. By the time I realized it, I thought you'd moved on."

"I loved you, Lauren." Part of him still did no matter how much he tried to deny it. "I would have done anything to make our marriage work."

She slipped past him and leaned against the door post, her arms wrapped around her waist the only clue that she wasn't as composed as she tried to appear. "I'm sorry. I'm sorry about not trusting you, about not talking to you—not telling you what was going on in my head."

Did her apology help ease the hurt? He did a mental check. Nope. That goddamned ache in his chest still hurt like a sonovabitch.

He forced himself to look at her without allowing her to see how much her apology hurt. He'd be damned if he'd give her that power over him. "I'm going back to D.C. Troy can—"

"Please. Don't leave." She moved closer, her breasts brushing his shirt, her hips touching his. She hadn't put on any perfume but there was still a hint of something fruity wafting from her, probably her shampoo.

His cock punched a tent in the front of his sweats. Fuck.

"Don't leave. Not with this still between us," she whispered. "I thought I was doing the right thing. Once I realized what a mess I'd made of things, I'd been told you were already with someone else and I figured it was better to let you go."

God, he wanted to touch her. To hold her. To have her rest her head against his shoulder the way she had the night before. While his brain was saying "damned straight I didn't understand," his cock was saying "lie down on the couch, babe, and let me taste you again." At the moment, it was a dead heat as to which body part would win the argument. Then his guts weighed in. When this was over—whatever *it* was—would he find himself alone? Because there was no way he could go through losing her again.

"How would you know if I was with someone else? You were half the fuckin' world away." Maybe if he couldn't smell her he could fight whatever spell she was weaving. Distance, that's what he needed. Yet he couldn't move; his legs felt like they'd been nailed in place. "What do you want from me, Lauren?"

"*From* you? Nothing. But I need to make things right for you, for both of us," she whispered. Her eyes slowly lifted to his again. He lost himself in the flecks of gold buried amongst the brown. "I want to...I want us to try again."

His hand reached for her, hovered an inch above her hair before he stopped himself. Damn, she looked just like she did when they were first dating. When they'd finally admitted what they'd each needed, wanted from the other. On their wedding day when she'd promised to love him for better or worse. Well, he sure as hell had delivered the worst, hadn't he?

She looked up at him, conviction firm in her voice as well as her eyes. "I'll do whatever you ask to prove myself to you. Except leave."

"Will you?" He gave in to the temptation and touched her hair with one finger. It was as soft, as silky as he remembered. He cupped the back of her head, holding her in place, letting her feel his control. A dark wave of lust swamped him. Why not make her prove she'd changed? Or not. Why not satisfy that demon inside that needed to punish her? He tightened his grip. "If I told you to suck me off right here where my men could see you, would you do it?"

"Yes." There was no hesitation to her answer. She started to reach for his waistband.

What the hell was he doing? They were out in the open where anyone could see. He had to work with these men, command their respect, not give them a thrill watching their boss get a blowjob. "Stop."

"But…"

Telling his dick it would just have to wait, he stepped out of her reach. "You want to do something for me? You want me to trust you? Then stop lying to me and tell me the truth. About what the hell the threat is and exactly why you're here."

They stared at each other for a long moment, the faint buzz of a plane thirty thousand feet above and a sparrow chirping to his mate the only sounds breaking the silence. Finally she nodded. "All right, but I can't tell you everything. Some of it's classified."

Classified? Perhaps this Light Brigade place she'd worked for had involved one of the alphabet agencies if Harris had terrorist connections. "Come on, let's go back to the house. I'd rather not have anyone listen in to whatever we end up saying."

Or watch whatever they ended up doing. Be it yelling or making love.

CHAPTER TEN

THE TWO OF THEM walked along the path back to the house without speaking. While they walked, Chad wondered if Lauren was composing answers for him with the same deliberation he was preparing his questions. For years he'd been composing what he wanted to ask. Yet so many of the questions now seemed futile or petty. She'd walked away from him. She'd been clear she hadn't agreed with his decision about the FBI. She'd been furious when that video of the two of them having sex in their bedroom had been posted on the internet and gone viral, how stills had been splashed across every goddamned newspaper on the east coast and beyond. To this day he figured out how someone had managed to sneak a camera into the house. He'd gone over the place with every detector he could lay his hands on and never found a trace of the goddamned thing.

He'd done every damned thing she'd asked. Yet it hadn't been enough. The sense of hope that had flared to life twisted on him, turned into a serpent intent on destroying his dreams.

Once they were in her room and he'd closed the door, Lauren took a deep breath and faced him. "I really am sorry. About leaving you. I know it was wrong. I apologize for that."

"You've said that already." He scrubbed his hands over his face as he fought for control. "Look, I know you were unhappy. I know you didn't agree with some of the choices I made. Thalia told me—"

"Let's not talk about Thalia right now." The bleakness in her eyes sucker punched him, driving away the righteous indignation that had driven him just moments before. "Even before Emily's death, I was pretty messed up. There was something wrong with me, about the way I watched Emily."

What had he missed? He thought back on those months, of watching her nursing Emily, cuddling her, sleeping with her right beside their bed, her hand often resting on their daughter as the two of them slept. "Babe, you were the best mother a baby could ever ask for. You were always there with Emily. You carried her everywhere you went. I know. I saw you."

"From the day we brought Em home from the hospital, I was terrified to go to sleep." Her voice cracked. "I was afraid if I did, she'd stop breathing and I wouldn't know."

How could that be? How could he not have seen that she'd been afraid? Then again he'd been at work during the day, a lot of evenings too. Especially that last month when he and his team had been winding up that inside trading investigation. Had he neglected his family because of a goddamned greedy banker? "During the day, when you were at work, I'd keep her in her carry seat, so I could take her with me everywhere. I was afraid to leave her alone." Her voice was a toneless whisper. "Then one day, she turned over on her own."

He remembered that day. She'd called him with the news but he'd had to cut her off because they were in the middle of a meeting. She'd been upset with him that night—at the time he'd thought she was angry because she felt he'd blown her off. Had it been fear driving her anger? "That's one of the signs she was growing up, Lauren. It meant she was healthy, that's all."

"They told us at our Lamaze classes we shouldn't let the baby sleep on her stomach, remember?" He stayed very still, afraid to jar her from her trance-like recitation. "After that, I was terrified. How was I supposed to stop her from rolling over on her stomach if I fell asleep?" She closed her eyes for a moment and took another deep breath. When she opened them again, her voice was steadier, controlled. At what cost? "I'd sit on the side of the bed with my hand on her, making sure she was breathing. Sometimes I'd watch her all night."

Oh, God, it was right in front of him and he hadn't seen it.

"I knew something was wrong with me, but I couldn't do anything, I couldn't say anything to anyone. I just kept hoping you'd see it. That you'd see what was happening and do something. Take me to the doctor or something."

"Why didn't say something? Tell me? I would have helped you."

"Because I was afraid. I terrified they'd say I was an unfit mother. That you'd take Emily away from me."

"I would never have taken her from you, babe. You loved her more than life itself." He couldn't help himself; he wrapped his arms about her and drew her close, stroking up and down her spine, gently, comforting the way she liked.

"That night. You came home late, remember?" Her whole body shuddered in his arms. "You'd wrapped some case up and got your promotion."

Oh, shit, and she'd fallen asleep after they'd made love. Had she never fallen asleep after the way he did? "Is that why you said it was my fault Emily...died?"

She took a deep shuddering breath, giving him the impression that she was ready to shatter. "Don't you see? If I'd been awake, I might have noticed that she'd stopped breathing. I might have been able to save her. I know it wasn't your fault, but I wasn't thinking straight and I…"

"It wasn't your fault. You know that. It wasn't anyone's fault." Here he'd been blaming himself, thinking Lauren had blamed him for Emily's death, and she'd been blaming herself. They'd both carried too much crap around for too long.

Her words were muffled but controlled. "Maybe I sensed something but just didn't realize it. If I'd said something, they could have tested her. Put her on one of those apnea blankets that monitored her breathing. If she'd been on one of those, the alarm would have gone off and we could have saved her."

Her head shook against his shoulder and he realized there was a damp patch on it. She was crying without making a sound. He held her tightly against him, stroking her back. "You can't second guess yourself, babe." He wore the crown of perfect vision hindsight after Thalia's shooting. He pulled Lauren away and cradled her face in his palms. Tears streaked down her face. He brushed his thumb over her cheek, wiping them from their tracks. "Emily had none of the indicators—she wasn't premature, she had no physical signs to make us suspect she'd stop breathing. You know that."

Lauren started to say something but he cut her off. "You read the autopsy report, Lauren. You know what the coroner said. You didn't do anything wrong. Neither of us did."

"I'm sorry," she whispered, her voice hoarse, as if she'd been shouting for hours. Her deep shuddering sigh echoed through his bones and settled into his soul.

He continued to stroke her cheek as the tears slowed. "So you ran to England?"

To Tranquil Pastures…which was a fancy name for a private clinic specializing in treating people having…mental difficulties. Oh, God. "You weren't in charge of security at that spa, were you?"

"No. I was a patient."

"Why didn't you tell me? Why not find something local?" Somewhere I could have visited you. Helped you.

"Thalia found the place for me. I told her I wanted it to be somewhere private so no one could find out that I was there. The press were already tearing you apart. I didn't want anyone to go after you because I was so weak." The press had been in a feeding frenzy and were pointing the fingers at him as the poster child of how the FBI had failed the country. What woman—especially one recovering from the death of her child—voluntarily put themselves into a spotlight like that? He wondered who had been advising her. His lawyers perhaps? Or Thalia?

And why the fuck hadn't Thalia told him where Lauren was or what she'd been going through? He didn't need to ask how his sister had raised the money. He had a damned good idea where it had come from—she'd been millionaire Cooper Davis's lover at the time. But however she'd gotten ahold of the cash, his sister was due for a long talk about boundaries, and secret keeping, and interfering between a husband and wife.

He started at the ceiling for a second before shaking his head and looking at her. "I get that you needed help. That you needed to get away from the press. From everything." His voice had thickened so he cleared his throat. "What I don't understand is why you stayed away for so long. Without a phone call. A letter. Something. Anything."

"I did write to you," Lauren said in confusion. "I wrote to you a couple weeks after I left, explaining where I was, begging your forgiveness. I wrote week after week. Asking you if I could come back when I was released. But you never replied. So when I got out, I didn't think you wanted me back."

"I didn't get any letters, Lauren. Not one."

HE HADN'T SEEN HER LETTERS? Oh, dear God, had Thalia been intercepting his mail? But on which end? At the spa or their condo? "I sent dozens."

He shook his head.

"I should have come back right then, shouldn't I?" She sighed. So many mistakes she'd made. Too many. "Then, one day, your lawyer showed up on my doorstep with the divorce papers. I took that as your answer, so I signed them." She debated telling him about Thalia's role, but decided against it. He'd figure it out soon enough. The conversation needed to be about them, not his sister.

"*My* lawyer showed up with the divorce papers?" His eyes closed and he canted his head back as he drew in a deep breath. When he looked at her again, his expression was shuttered. "You divorced me, Lauren. Not the other way around. I'm the one who got served."

"No, I didn't seek the divorce. I'd wanted to come home, to try again. I swear." Dear God, he didn't believe her. Lauren's legs wouldn't support her; she slumped onto the bed. "The solicitor said he represented your lawyers here in the States. He said you were living with someone else. That you wanted the divorce so you could marry her."

"What was the solicitor's name?" Chad's voice was soft, but she heard the menace underlying it.

She told him, wondering just what Chad would do to him. Destroy his career? Or have him met in a dark corner someplace to mete out his own form of vengeance?

"It wasn't until a few weeks ago that I discovered you'd never remarried." *That you weren't the one who had hired the lawyer.*

His breath escaped him in a huff; he looked to the side. "I kept hoping you'd come back. I bought a house and fixed it up. So if you came back I could offer you somewhere better to live than our condo. And I own forty-nine percent of Hauberk, Lauren. Sam's my partner, not my boss." The look he gave her was so bleak her chest ached. "I did it for you, Lauren. I know I fucked up with the FBI. I know you were disappointed with me for going against orders, that you didn't think I'd be able to provide for you anymore. I needed to prove to you that I could still be someone you could rely on."

"I never thought that. Oh, God, Chad, I never ever thought that of you. I know why you went against orders. I understand that. I always did." She closed the distance between them and wrapped her arms about his waist. "I didn't leave you because of that."

His arms banded around her, holding her tight against him. How long they stood there she couldn't say. Eventually he took a deep breath and placed his hands on her shoulders, pulling her away.

"We've both made mistakes. That ends now. We say whatever we feel, we don't shut the other out and expect them to know what we're thinking. Agreed?"

She nodded. Half of her hoped Harris wouldn't be found for months. Hell, ninety-nine-point-nine percent of her hoped Harris would never be found. They could live here forever, safe.

CHAD WRAPPED HIS ARMS around Lauren and pulled her against him once more. She sighed with a quiet moan as she softened against him.

This was the way it was supposed to be. The two of them together, damn the world outside. If she hadn't sought the divorce the way he'd believed, and she hadn't left...was there hope for them?

There was so much time to make up, so many nights he'd been alone with only his own hand to satisfy his needs. The nights he'd spent on duty at the club, watching everyone else having sex hadn't helped. In the years they'd been together, she'd known how to turn him on, known that he didn't like a passive woman but a willing partner. Her heart hammered against his chest, her breath warmed his cheek in a gentle caress, her hips ground against his erection.

He lowered his head and caught her lips in a kiss, one with enough pressure that she'd know exactly what he expected.

Her fingernails digging into his biceps was his first clue that she remembered. And that she'd give him exactly what he needed. He damned near swore when her grip on him ceased until his sweat pants slid down his legs to pool at his ankles. She broke the kiss and sank to her knees.

Was there anything as erotic as watching her tongue dart out to dampen her lips, or the smoky look in her eyes as she stared at his erection?

Her mouth closed over the swollen tip and he had to say yes, having her mouth sucking his cock was a lot more fucking erotic. Her tongue slid up the length of his shaft and her hand circled the base in a loose fist.

"Suck it down, babe. You know how I like it."

She did. God, her mouth hadn't lost any of its skill. She used just the right pressure with her tongue, her teeth rasped just the right spots and the suction that hollowed out her cheeks...holy fucking shit. Her free hand slipped around his ass, cupping one of his cheeks. When she started humming, the vibration shot straight down his shaft and landed in his balls.

He groaned from deep in his belly and wrapped his fingers in her hair. She rocked against him, taking him deep until the head hit the soft palate at the back of her mouth, then withdrew. She repeated the movement until he clung to her as if the room was spinning. His eyelids weighed a ton. He fought them from closing. If they did, she might disappear and he'd wake up to find this was all a dream.

The familiar tingle started in his balls, drawing them up tight against this body and he stopped her.

"On the bed, babe. I need to finish inside you."

She withdrew, taking the time to press a kiss to the end of his glistening shaft in a gesture so sweet, so gentle, he wanted to gather her in his arms and just hold her. How had he ever let her just walk away? Why hadn't he flown to London to visit her, to find out… No, he told himself. Those days were past, and while he knew there were questions still to be answered, this was not the time. If nothing else came of this reunion, he'd have the memory of her beneath him, around him one last time.

A frown creased her forehead. "I should have a shower. I'm all sweaty."

"So am I. I don't care." He pulled his T-shirt over his head and dropped it on his sweat pants then reached for her shirt.

Their clothes on the floor seconds later, Lauren stretched out on the bed, propping herself up on the pillows. His chest tightened as her hand smoothed over her belly and she parted her folds and began to play with herself. His cock ached to be inside her, especially when she let her legs fall open and gave him a glimpse of her glistening pussy. Shit, she knew how he loved watching her get herself off. But watching would have to wait.

He crawled up the bed and wedged himself between her thighs. God, he'd loved how she smelled, how she tasted. Her scent had lingered in the closet for a few weeks, no more, and he'd mourned when it had faded. He buried his face in her mound and inhaled, filling his lungs with her.

Ignoring the need to continue his path up her body, he stayed right where he was. He deserved the chance to reacquaint himself with this part of her body. Besides, while he was primed and ready, she'd had no foreplay at all.

He nuzzled lower until her essence coated his lips. Her taste burst on his tongue like a ripened peach. He swirled his tongue through her cream, alternately lapping and teasing until he found the tiny bundle of nerves. Her hips rose off the mattress but he clamped down, holding her in place.

He'd intended to hold off on finding his own pleasure until she'd come for him twice, but she moaned that deep-throated gasp that forewarned him of an impending orgasm and all his plans flew out the window. He found himself over her, his cock poised at her entrance. Her legs wrapped about his thighs and drew him close until he was buried to the hilt inside her.

None of his dreams, none of his memories, matched the sheer heaven of being surrounded by her heat. He stared down at her, wanting to order her to open her eyes, to watch them unfocus as she came. But there was something ethereal about the look on her face that made him hold off. He didn't need to see her eyes when her body told her everything he needed to know. Her swollen lips were parted, tiny puffs of air as she gasped for breath warmed his arm when she turned her head, unseeing, toward it. Her body rippled around him, drawing him in deeper. Her hips undulated, grinding her clit with each pass. Her nipples were hard dark berries, larger than they had been when they were first married, softer too, from age and breast feeding but they were just as beautiful.

He dipped his head and caught one between his teeth. He wanted to crow when her pussy clamped tight around him. When this was over he'd ask her about the scar on the inside part of her arm that looked like a burn or the one on her hip where a bullet had gone in one fleshy side and out the other. For now, he'd celebrate that they were here. Together.

He rocked his hips back then pushed back in, balls deep. His own eyes closed as he set a steady rhythm, until he could control himself no more. Her heels dug into his behind and her nails dug into his biceps as she came silently. When he followed her seconds later, he wasn't so quiet, his hoarse roar echoing off the walls.

It took him a moment before he could rouse himself to roll off her. As soon as he was on the mattress beside her, Lauren rolled into his arms with a murmured, "I love you" that had him closing his eyes and burying his face in her hair.

Maybe they could make it work. For the first time in years, hope replaced the dark pressure in his heart.

CHAPTER ELEVEN

LAUREN AWOKE TO FIND Chad wrapped around her the way he had for the last four nights. Like each previous morning, his hand rested on her breast while his erection prodded her hip. "Mmm, that's a nice way to wake up."

"Just relax, babe. Let me do all the work." The heat of his breath on her skin was the only warning she got before he sucked her nipple into his mouth. He spent a few minutes toying with her, his teeth rasping over her delicate flesh, occasionally tugging with a sharp nip, then his tongue would soothe the sting until she was panting.

She shifted, with every intention of touching him, but her hands wouldn't move. Another tug confirmed it—he'd restrained her wrists above her head while she slept. Had he restrained her ankles too? She wiggled her feet. Nope. Well, this should be…interesting.

Squinting, she opened her eyes, letting them adjust to the bright sunlight slanting across the bed that painted his skin pure gold. "You mind telling me just how long you plan on keeping me here?"

Tell me "forever."

He lifted his head and looked at her, a wolfish look in his eyes and a smile tugging at his lips. "I don't plan on loosening those restraints until I've made you come at least three times."

"You've always loved a challenge."

He set to his task, using his mouth and his hands to rediscover all the places that drove her crazy—the spot on her neck directly beneath her ear, the soft skin inside her elbow, just above each hip. She closed her eyes and gave in to the erotic sensation of his breath and his mouth on her. He explored every inch of her body until she was panting, aching with need.

Finally he parted her folds with his thumbs. His tongue traced where his thumbs had been, flicking over her clit with a light touch.

"I've always loved how you taste, Lauren." When they'd been married and he said that, there had been pride in his voice, but now…now there was need, heat, urgency. And something else. Not anger, but… determination? Whether to prove something to her or to him, she didn't even try to guess. Before she could decide how she felt, he returned to his task. Her orgasm slammed into her like a tidal wave, lifting her hips from the mattress as her pussy sought to be filled.

He planted his hands on either side of her head and eased into her. She lost herself in the familiarity of the scene. Of his scent, his rhythm. Him surrounding her. Filling her. The sounds of flesh on flesh, their breathing as it quickened, became her whole world. *This. This is what I've searched for. This is what I missed, what I've wanted.*

He'd just collapsed on top of her, both having found their release, when someone knocked at Chad's bedroom door.

"Do you think if we're quiet they'll go away?" she whispered. She felt Chad's snort more than heard it.

The handle to Chad's door rattled. On the far side there was a quiet curse, then whoever it was pounded on her door. "Get your butt out here, Miller." Troy. Shit. "Sam's on the phone."

"All right, I'm coming," Chad called in return.

"Not anymore," Lauren said beneath her breath. Even exhausted from their lovemaking as she was, she couldn't help but admire his butt when he rolled out of bed and headed to the bathroom.

When he returned, he leaned against the doorframe. She tugged on the restraints still binding her to the headboard. "Do you mind letting me go? I could use a trip to the bathroom myself."

Her chest hurt at the predatory satisfaction of the smile he gave her. "I'm not sure. I'm not done yet, am I?"

"What do you mean?"

"I told you I'd make you come three times and by my count you've only come twice."

"You always were an overachiever." Her breath caught when he leaned down to kiss her. Without breaking the kiss, he freed her, allowing her to wrap her arms around his neck. They were both breathing heavily before he broke away. "Promise me you'll come back and give me a chance to even the score?"

"I won't be long. And I will definitely be back. You can count on it."

"Chad." Troy pounded on the door again. "Get your ass out here before I break the effin' door, damnit."

He returned to his room and closed the adjoining door. Lauren swung from the bed and padded to the bathroom. When she returned, the connecting door was open once again. Instead of Chad, Troy stood in the middle of the room, his expression guarded as his gaze raked the length of her.

"Well, well, well. Looks like Father Christmas arrived early—or late—this year. You look good with your hair all messed up like that. The razor burn on your chest is a nice touch too."

She headed to the closet to grab a robe, then stopped. Chad had said he would be right back and she was damned if she'd let Troy stop him from giving her that third orgasm. Instead she grabbed the top sheet off the bed and wrapped it around her toga style. "Where's Chad?"

"Talking to Sam on the encrypted system downstairs. He'll be back in a bit." His gaze met hers finally, his expression hard. "The longer you play kissy-face while lying to him, the worse it's going to hurt him when he finds out the truth. Just get it over with—tell him. Tell him everything.

"He knows about why I was at the spa."

"Good." He nodded in approval. "Then tell him the rest. About the Brigade. And about Thalia's part in committing you to that asylum."

She stilled. "You know what she did?"

"I overheard that fight you had with her, remember? About how she'd told you Chad had remarried." Troy had been the one who had told her Chad barely even dated. "I also told you, I got into your files, remember? After I read yours, I read hers."

"Oh."

"You need to tell him, Lauren. He needs to know."

"What am I supposed to say? 'By the way, Chad, your sister is a lying bitch who manipulated me and I was so stupid I let her'?"

"He deserves the truth, damn it. Not many men these days live with the type of code he holds himself and others to. If you want to keep him, you'll effin' come clean to him. He deserves that much after what he's given up for you both. He gave up his career to protect her."

"Going against orders was his choice." The hurt, the betrayal she'd felt when she'd learned what he'd done raked her again. Not that he'd gone against them, but that he hadn't talked to her first. But even if she'd known, what would she have said or done? "He could have asked her to stop going to that damned place until Vandeburg was captured."

"He had. She refused."

Lauren stilled. "He never told me."

Troy sighed. "All right, so save Thalia for later. For Christ's sake, at least tell him who Cooper really is and have him banned from that damned club before he brings trouble to its doors. That's the last thing either Sam or Chad need after sacrificing their careers for it."

"Yes, Lauren. Tell me who Cooper really is. Tell me why he should be banned from his own club."

Her own expression couldn't have looked any less guilty than Troy's when they both stared at Chad, who stood in the connecting doorway.

Tension radiated from him as he stalked into the room, his fingers flexing as if they wanted to go for his weapon. Or punch Troy in the jaw. When he looked at her, the warmth that had been in them just minutes before had been replaced with ice.

"Who the hell is Cooper, Lauren? What's he doing that should get him banned from the club?" Chad repeated.

Troy's shoulders slumped; he ran a hand through his thick mane of hair. "Cooper's running—"

"Troy, stop," Lauren interrupted, sensing he was quite willing to throw her to the wolves. "I'm sorry, Chad, but Troy can't tell you anything about it. You need to forget what you just heard."

The glare he turned on her could have withered a nun's wimple. "Like hell I'm going to forget what I heard. Now, you tell me what Cooper's up to."

"We can't."

"You won't," Chad corrected.

"No, I mean we can't. We signed a secrecy agreement."

"What'll happen if you break that agreement? You'll be slapped on the wrist? Fired? You've told me you've already quit." His voice could have frozen the Potomac in July. "What the hell is he doing? Is Cooper the man you were investigating? Is he the one who hired Harris?"

When she didn't answer, he yelled, "Tell me, damn it!"

"Cooper is my boss. That's all I can tell you. And even that can get us all in trouble."

Troy apparently didn't feel the same boundaries. "Fuck that. Cooper is head of The Brigade. It's a multi-government, black-op, hostage rescue unit that operates separately from any of the government agencies in order to provide plausible deniability."

CHAPTER TWELVE

CHAD JERKED BACK as if he'd been shot. He straightened and looked between the two of them, processing the various scenarios from the little information he'd gleaned and added it to his conversation with Sam. "You lied to me. Both of you."

"We had to," Lauren agreed quietly. "The Brigade often has to infiltrate terrorist organizations. If the wrong piece of information gets out, if the wrong person finds out about something, people could die. If we talk to someone who we're not authorized to talk to, we can be charged with treason and tried in a very private court with a very private—and very final—sentence."

His stomach felt as if he'd been buckled into a roller coaster that was doing loops and spins, ready to rocket off its rails. He hated roller coasters.

He glanced at Troy, who was staring stone-faced out the window. "How long have you known about this?"

"About eight months. It was the Brigade who extracted our guys in Colombia." Troy slumped on the windowsill. "Lauren was running the op. I don't remember seeing Weir there, but things got pretty hairy and…well, maybe he was there and I just missed him."

"Does Sam know about any of this?"

"No. And you can't tell him."

The roller coaster they were riding flipped over in a dozen different directions then abruptly stopped. She'd owed him no explanation. If she'd been working with a black ops team, she wouldn't have been able to tell him anything. They'd each had to keep certain parts of their work secret from each other before. How was this any different?

Troy was a different matter. He may have possibly put not only Hauberk but the club members at risk.

However there was nothing to be done about it at the moment. Not until they'd solved this current situation.

"Is there really a threat? Is there really a Jack Harris?"

"Yes, Jack Harris is real. He's after me because I had him taken off active duty. And you're a target because he may try to get back at me through you."

Could he believe her? She'd given him a completely different story in the gazebo. Was this tale any closer to the truth than that one? "Who is he really?"

"He's a former British agent. He'd been working undercover to infiltrate an offshoot of the Shining Path when his cover got blown. He didn't like the way his government handled his case after he got back so Cooper recruited him."

"Why did you have him taken off active duty?"

She took a deep breath. "I can't tell you everything, but I can tell you we noticed he was having problems after a mission went sour in Somalia."

"PTSD?"

She nodded. "Among other things."

Somalia, with its war lords and lawlessness. She'd been facing those thugs? Chad pinched the bridge of his nose. Too many scenarios flashed through his mind. Too many questions. Troy had said Colombia had been a hell of a firefight; where else had she been? "Were you in charge of the op that went bad? Is that why he's after you?"

"No, I was in charge of his next mission. He wigged out and damned near caused us all to be killed. When we got back Cooper put him on administrative leave. Because I was the one who signed the report, he's focused on me as being the cause of all his problems."

"A variation of the 'kill the messenger' response." He'd seen it before. "Was Weir part of the decision making process?"

"No. Ed was part of the team, but I'm the only one he's targeting."

"I wouldn't be so sure about that." There was no way to break it to her gently, and no time either.

"Weir's dead, Lauren."

Beside him, Troy swore and turned away. Lauren said nothing but color drained from her face.

"He was found this morning in a seedy hotel room up near Fredrick. According to the news reports, other guests reported hearing an argument in the middle of the night and called the front desk. When the police arrived, the room had been trashed and Weir was dead. His throat had been slit." He narrowed his eyes at Lauren's curse.

He shared a confused look with Troy when she knelt at the side of the bed and stuck her hand between the box spring and mattress. "Lauren? What are you looking for?"

"The transponder."

"The what?" He took a step forward at the same time as Troy.

"A transponder—Ed gave it to me in case things went bad here and I needed to be extracted."

"You didn't have any sort of device with you." Troy's eyes were wide with horror when he met Chad's glance. "I swear, we checked. Walters went over her with a wand before they took off the first time, and we checked again right after I met her. We took her purse away, everything. There were no devices on her. I swear."

LAUREN SAT BACK ON HER HEELS and stared at the device she'd retrieved. It was smaller than the key fob Chad used to unlock his car doors. "Ed tucked it in my hair just before he left. Andy was thorough but you…"

"Just checked your fucking clothes," Troy snarled.

From the look on Troy's face, Chad was pretty sure if he hadn't been in the room Troy might have attacked Lauren.

Her fingers closed around the device. "Don't worry, it doesn't broadcast its location unless it's turned on. Which it hasn't been since I arrived. So if Harris took the other unit from Ed, he can't find me." She placed it on the floor. "We have to destroy this one so there's no chance it can ever broadcast our location. Troy, stomp on it. Break the damned thing."

"No. Don't," Chad barked when Troy took a step forward. "We might be able to use it to draw Harris in."

It was almost comical the way both Troy's and Lauren's expression mirrored identical looks of understanding within a split second of each other.

"We set him up." Troy scooped up the transponder and started pacing, toying with it with each step. "We choose a place we can watch without him realizing it. Make him think Lauren's there. Catch him in the act of breaking in."

"There's always the chance he may not have Ed's device or the right codes," Lauren said.

Chad shook his head. "Someone's going to know if it's among Weir's things. Sam said there was a single report on the news this morning but nothing since. Someone is keeping a lid on it." Which meant Davis had a helluva lot of connections to keep the press muzzled.

"Andy might be able to find out if it's missing through his police buddies," Troy suggested. "In the meantime, I'll take this effin' thing back to D.C. and set something up with Cooper so he can...*neutralize* Harris nice and quiet."

"We'll be fine with Andy in charge of things up here." Chad stopped Troy before he could leave the room. "When I came in, you two were talking about the club being used as a front. Lauren, will Harris be looking for you there?"

Lauren hesitated. "I don't think Harris knew anything about the club. There was some emergency going on that Cooper couldn't get away from, so he had Ed and I meet him there. It was one time only. I don't think any of the other team members knew about it, or would connect it with the group."

It didn't quite add up. If it was only used the one time, why refer to it as a front? "Tell me no one in the club has ever been put into any sort of danger."

"No." But doubt fluttered about the edges of her response. Shit, he had to get word out. Make sure Thalia stayed away. Sam and Rosie too.

"Is it possible Harris will go after Cooper himself?"

Lauren pursed her lips for a second before shaking her head. "Cooper's deliberately created opportunities for Harris to go after him if he wanted. As far as we can tell, Harris is fixated on me."

"Have you told me everything I should know about it?"

There was a split second's hesitation to her "yes" this time. Shit. Shit. SHIT.

"I've told you everything I'm allowed to tell you," she finally allowed.

His suspicions settled down at her answer. Somewhat. Rules and secrets were part of his world. And hers. "Is there anything you're not telling me that might affect how we've set up the protection of this place? Or of the club?"

"No." No hesitation.

All right, he could live with that. As long as she was telling him the truth. "When this is over, you and I are going to sit down and have a long talk."

Troy snorted. "Since you're both stuck here until we stop Harris, I'd say you two could start talking now."

He turned on Troy. "Before you start casting stones, you might want to remember that you've known about this for almost a year and not said anything. So don't go postal on Lauren for keeping quiet." Troy had the good grace to look away.

Chad rolled his shoulders, releasing the tension that had been building in them. "All right. Let's plan what we're going to do to draw him in. The sooner we can get it underway the sooner we can get out of here."

CHAPTER THIRTEEN

LAUREN SHIFTED HER WEIGHT between the balls of her feet, watching for an opening. When she saw it, she brought up her knee and snapped her foot out, aiming toward Chad's solar plexus. Perhaps she'd telegraphed what she was going to do, or maybe she shouldn't have tried it twice in a row because this time he deflected the kick and spun away.

"You always did have a nice roundhouse."

"Thanks." She raised her hands and started circling again, allowing herself to admire the play of his shoulder muscles. Muscles that had rippled beneath her fingers the night before. The quick jab she took at him didn't make it past his glove.

For the next two minutes there was only the smack of leather on leather, and the occasional grunt when a hit connected, interrupting the silence of the gym. Then Chad telegraphed what she thought was going to be a right cross. Turned out it was a feint and he landed a forward kick to her solar plexus. She would have cursed him. If she could have drawn a breath.

"Shit! I tried to pull it but you leaned in." He grabbed her under her arms and held her so her lungs could fill with the air he'd knocked from her.

She hauled in a breath, then another. "Good one."

"Thanks."

Covered in sweat from her workout, Lauren stripped as she followed Chad to the bathroom. "Mind if I join you?"

The dark look he gave her sent a thrill down her spine and into her very core. "I'd be disappointed if you didn't."

He turned on the shower then stripped off his tee. Lauren frowned when he folded it before putting it in the hamper. She'd noticed that about him before—from the way his clothes were arranged in his closet, to how everything on his desk was neat and tidy. Even tidier than hers. "What's up with the neat freak routine all of a sudden? Did you have a housekeeper who complained about how you left your clothes on the floor the way you did when we were married?"

The heat in his eyes changed to ice, as did his tone. "There's no pleasing you, is there? When we were married, you'd complain that you were always having to pick up after me, and now I put things away properly, you're questioning me?"

Tread carefully. "I just wondered what changed—you never used to worry about dropping your clothes on the floor or leaving papers piled up on the desk..."

"What changed?" He advanced on her until they were inches apart. "You left. That's what changed."

Oh God. He didn't mean..."You thought if you kept things cleaner, if you hung up your clothes, I'd come back?" She reached up and stroked his neck. "Chad, I didn't leave you because you left your clothes on the floor. You know that, don't you?"

He shook his head. "All I knew was you weren't there anymore." He rested his forehead against hers. "I knew you were upset that I didn't talk to you about going against orders to protect Thalia but I couldn't go back into the past and change it."

"So you changed what you could." She wrapped her arms around him and laid her head on his shoulder. He stayed tense for a moment then relaxed and held her too. "We were both trying to change things in our own way, weren't we? To fix things we couldn't fix."

"I was willing to do anything I could to get you back."

She knew that feeling. After all, she'd spent years running, fixing up other people's messes, living from a suitcase while leaving no traces of herself wherever she went. How she wished there was some magic time machine...but there wasn't. "I know we can't go back, but is there a future for us?" *When this is over, will I lose you again?*

His brows drew together in that familiar way.

"We have a lot to work out. I know there are things you're still not telling me."

She dropped her gaze. "You know I signed—"

"I'm not talking about your agreement with the Brigade. There's something else you're not telling me, isn't there? Like the divorce that you think I asked you for while I think it was the other way around. About the letters that you sent me that I never got."

"There are going to be some things you may not want to hear. I need you to trust me about some of the rest. That there may be things that I'm protecting you from."

"Did you remarry? Has there been someone else?"

She hid her relief at his gruff tone. He was jealous. "No. There's never been anyone else."

He fell silent for a moment but she didn't dare break the spell. "Remember I said I bought a house? I've spent a lot of time fixing it up—I've put in hardwood floors and torn out a lot of '70s paneling. I put in a new kitchen too."

She knew that already. Except Thalia had told her he'd bought it with his new wife. "I'd like to see it one day."

"You don't have to share a bedroom with me, but I've got one to spare. If you'd like." That would last for…a minute. "I'd like that."

Footsteps slapped across the mats, slowed then stopped at the door. A half-second later, someone knocked. "You two decent in there?"

"Come on in."

Andy stuck his head in, his gaze taking a long sweep down Lauren's form that had a growl forming in Chad's throat.

"What do you want?"

"Troy called. The setup worked. They caught Harris attempting to break into the decoy home. He ate a bullet rather than be arrested." He tossed Lauren's cellphone to them; Chad caught it handily. "He says Lauren's boss wants to talk to you both."

CHAPTER FOURTEEN

LAUREN PULLED THE RENTAL CAR into the driveway of a modest two-story Colonial Chad had directed her to. It was the type they used to drive by and say *some day, we'll own a house like that.* A massive beech tree shaded the front lawn, though its leaves now covered the lawn not the branches. She could picture Chad playing catch with a son, or daughter, beneath it. Or maybe he'd put up a hoop over the two-car garage and teach their child how to free throw. If she even dared thinking about having another child.

One hurdle at a time.

"You're right. It's just the type of house we used to dream about." She pulled the keys from the ignition and pressed the button to release the trunk latch.

"I'll get it," he said calmly when she reached for the door handle.

Ever the gentleman, he walked around the car and held open the door for her. She took the hand he offered to help her out—it wasn't that she needed the help. Or maybe, from the way her knees were shaking, she did.

Lauren tightened the grip on her purse and followed him in, waiting in the open doorway while he turned off the alarm. A beam of late afternoon sunlight bounced off the crystal chandelier hanging from the two-story ceiling. The oak banister gleamed as if it had just been polished, as did the matching hardwood floor. "It's beautiful."

"Do you want a tour?" Chad had his hands stuck in his pockets again, a sign she remembered meant he was nervous. At least she wasn't the only one whose knees were beating a tattoo to rival a woodpecker.

She trailed him as he took her on a tour of the house. They started in the kitchen where she admired the glass-fronted units and granite counter then proceeded through the first floor—an office they could share, the living room with its marble-fronted fireplace and two-story wood-beamed ceilings.

"I hired an architect to redesign it," he explained when they reached the top floor. "It used to be a four bedroom but I had him combine one of the smaller bedrooms with the master. You'd always said you wanted an ensuite...I thought maybe..."

That if he'd made everything perfect, she'd come back to him. The same way he'd become almost obsessive about picking up his clothes and keeping things neat. "Show me?"

He held out his hand, waiting until she'd laced their fingers together before leading her to the master suite dominated by a king-sized bed.

"I can't tell you how long I've waited to show you this room. To..." He shook his head. "Never mind. One day at a time, right?"

Right about certain things. But not for what she sensed he needed. "To what? To make love to me? To tie me up and have your way with me the way we used to?"

"Yes." Need and desire filled both his voice and his eyes.

"So what are you waiting for? I'm here. Tell me what you want me to do."

"Take your clothes off." A command, not a question. A shiver of anticipation ran up her spine with heated fingers.

Dropping her purse on the floor, she removed her holster and placed it on the dresser. She slipped off her blouse, then unhooked her bra and let it fall beside her purse. Her slacks hit the floor moments later followed by her thin, lacy boy shorts. Her pulse jacked into the triple digits as she stood naked while he was completely clothed. The air in the room thinned and heated at the same time, especially as his gaze raked her.

"Play with yourself. Touch yourself the way you want me to touch you." His voice rasped over her skin, setting her nerve endings on fire as if he'd scraped her all over with sandpaper.

The way she wanted him to touch her? She let her head fall back and closed her eyes as she fondled her breasts. As she had so many times in the past, she imagined it was his fingers stroking the sensitive skin, tweaking her nipples.

"Don't close your eyes, Lauren. Look at me while you're pleasuring yourself."

Her eyelids were heavy but she forced them open and found he'd moved closer. She pinched her nipples hard enough to create a sting that soon changed to heat. *This, this is what I want you to do.* She tugged and rolled them again and again, the moisture below gathering as the sensation shot to her pussy.

Not breaking her gaze, one hand slipped over her belly and between her thighs. Cream drenched her fingers as they slid through her folds.

"Is that what you want me to do to you?"

"Yes."

He crowded her, so close the heat from his body warmed her over-sensitized skin. "My mouth or my fingers?"

"Either. Both." While her one hand continued to play with her breasts, her hips rotated, pressing her clit against her palm. She quickened her pace then needing more, plunged one finger, then another inside her. Each breath grew harder to draw. "Oh God, Chad, I want you inside me. Your fingers, your cock, I don't care. I need..."

Before she could push herself over the edge and climax, Chad grabbed her hand from between her legs. He lifted it to his mouth, sucking first one finger then the other. Once they were clean, he bent his head and captured one of her taut nipples with his teeth while his other hand ventured where hers had been.

LAUREN MOANED as he plunged his fingers inside her at the same time he nipped at her breast. The stinging caused by his teeth combined with the pleasure of his fingers until she had to hang onto his shoulders to remain upright. He varied the speed and the depth of his penetration, bringing her close to climax at least twice before he withdrew.

As much as she wanted to moan her complaint, to beg him to let her come, she kept her mouth shut. He took great pride in making her come multiple times, so whatever he had planned, she was prepared to wait him out.

"Kneel on the bed with your ass in the air."

She did as he bid, turning her head to watch him methodically strip. He removed his gun from its holster and placed it in the bedside table. Leaving her waiting was part of his plan she decided as he opened the closet and hung his suit jacket. Like at the farm, he folded his shirt and placed it in the hamper. She used the time to watch the play of muscles on his back and abdomen as he stripped his trousers and hung them on a press. When he was finally naked, his cock was still fully erect. Instead of returning to her, he headed into the bathroom.

She didn't have to ask what he was looking for—she'd known as soon as he'd turned her onto her stomach what he'd want. He returned a few moments later, his erection hard and tall against his belly.

Her eyes widened at the items he carried upon his return. The butt plug he placed on the mattress beside her was at least the same size as his cock so she wasn't too worried about it, but her pulse raced at the riding crop he set beside her.

He knelt behind her and murmured, "Spread your legs wider, babe."

She shuffled until her knees were the distance apart he'd indicated. As soon as she stopped moving, he picked up the bottle of lube and applied a generous dollop to the anal plug and coated it with his fingers. "Relax."

It was easier for him to say than for her to do, especially when he squirted lube over her behind. And even tougher when he pressed the hard tip of the plug against her opening. As he pressed it inward, his other hand toyed with her clit. Before she knew it, her hips were rotating against his fingers, her ass pressed against the plug and it popped past the ring of muscles. "Stand up, Lauren."

She carefully pushed herself to a stand. His features, normally so carefully controlled, were unguarded, the lust and desire filling his eyes, hardening his lips. He wanted her like this. He needed her.

As much as she needed him.

She stayed still as he fixed the harness to the plug and around her hips.

"Get back on the bed the way you were before. Grab hold of the headboard."

She bit her lip to keep herself from moaning and hurried to position herself the way he'd ordered. He'd not fastened the second cuff around her wrist securing her to the headboard, and she was already trembling in anticipation.

After laying a kiss on her shoulder, he set to work massaging her shoulders and working down her back with the skill of a trained masseuse. By the time he'd reached her hips, she'd forgotten about the restraints. Hell, her body had forgotten it had bones, she was so relaxed. If she'd been a cat, she'd have been purring.

He shifted his weight, parting her legs so he could kneel between them. His fingers trailed over the globes of her cheeks and down to her pussy. She just about purred when he dipped them into her opening and filled her. Between his thumb on her clit and his two fingers deep inside, he soon had her pressing back, her body heating as her second orgasm overtook her.

Until he picked up the riding crop she'd forgotten. He'd spanked her on occasion, a light tap on her behind, and she'd enjoyed it, but this…this was different. This would hurt.

He leaned over her, stroking the leather strip of the crop down her spine. Her body tensed, tightening around the butt plug until it felt massive.

"You either trust me." His fingers parted her folds and unerringly found her clit, toying with it until she was ready to agree to anything. Then he withdrew. "Or you don't."

If he'd wanted to seek revenge from her, wouldn't he have done that back at the farm? "Lauren?"

You either trust me or you don't. It was a test. She closed her eyes and nodded. "I trust you, Chad."

She'd barely finished speaking when the crop whistled across her left butt cheek. A second stroke followed the first, this one over the right buttock. While it initially stung, it didn't hurt. He struck each cheek twice more, then smoothed the sting with his hand. Once she realized it wouldn't hurt, he continued until her ass was on fire and her pussy dripped with her arousal.

He settled beneath her thighs, using his tongue on her clit, his fingers scissoring into her tight passage. Alternating between licking her clit and tugging on it with his lips, he took her to the brink of orgasm. She couldn't stop herself from crying out when he let her fly, her body clenching around his fingers and the plug, pulsing in ecstasy.

Her pussy hadn't stopped pulsing when he withdrew the plug leaving her feeling emptier than she could ever remember. Without giving her any warning, he thrust in hard, stretching her, the burning pain mixing with an unending pleasure of the remains of her last orgasm. Only he'd known what she liked, how she liked.

He tangled his fingers in her hair, pulling it until her head arched back. He withdrew and slammed back in again until she shuddered around him. "Do you feel how much I want you?"

"Yessss…" As much as she wanted him.

"Do you know I've never taken another woman here? That I've never wanted to?"

Realizing it was important to him, she found the breath to speak. "No one else has been there either."

At her confession, he slowed his thrusts with a groan. Moving ever so slowly he withdrew then returned.

She pressed her hips back against him, tightening her muscles, holding him in. His fingers dug into her hips as he gave into the pleasure. When he began a series of frenzied thrusts that pushed her closer and closer to the edge of her third orgasm, she buried her face in the sheets. God, how bland the last decade had been without the fire he'd brought to her, the strength of her orgasm rippled through her.

Moments later, Chad's cock pulsed deep inside her, his come heating her passage until every inch of her felt aflame. The sensation paled to the heat of his breath on her shoulder or his gasped "love you".

As soon as he fell on the mattress beside her, Lauren attempted to roll to him, to hold him only to be stopped by the bonds holding her in place.

Still breathing heavily, Chad cracked open an eye at her curses. "Hang on a sec."

He reached up and loosened the bindings, but not before he'd taken her breath away again with another deep kiss. Once she was free, he gathered her in his arms. Lauren would have been content to lie there for the rest of the night, to hold him and be held. Instead Chad slipped a hand beneath her knees and lifted her. "Come on, let's get cleaned up."

The ensuite bathroom he'd had designed was a work of art. Where he'd taken charge in the bedroom, she pressed him against the tiles and picked up a bar of soap. The room filled with steam from the multiple showerheads and the occasional soft murmur as they cleaned up. They both seemed to sense there was no need for words, simply being in the same room together again was enough. The last of the lather swirling down the drain, Lauren wrapped her arms around Chad's waist and rested her head on his shoulder. "I love you too."

His "hmm" of satisfaction turned into a chuckle when her stomach growled loudly enough to be heard over the water. "Do you want to go out for dinner tonight or order in?"

"In." Preferably something they could eat while sprawled naked on the bed.

He grabbed a towel from the rack and wrapped it around her, and tucked the end into her cleavage. Before he could wrap his towel around his hip, Lauren took it from him. She lingered over her task, patting every single part of him dry. The sun had long since set when they finally walked back into the bedroom. Chad flicked on the light. Before she could step around him, he'd shoved her behind him but she hit the doorframe with an oomph.

"Stay where you are, Mr. Miller." Shit, there was a man in their bedroom.

Chad held out his hands and adopted the reasonable tone they'd been taught during their hostage negotiation training at Quantico. "Tom? Put the gun down and let's talk about what you're doing here."

Gun. Her empty holster lay on the bed. Aw fuck. It was her own gun that Tom Whoever was using.

"I don't think so. I know you're hiding a whore behind you. You tell her to come out where I can see her." Lauren didn't recognize the voice, but being called a whore had her balling her fists.

"Tom, the woman behind me isn't a whore. It's my wife. You remember Lauren, don't you?"

It was someone they knew? Lauren peered over his shoulder. It startled her to recognize their intruder. The man she'd last seen as a fourteen-year-old boy now stood at least two inches taller than Chad. "Tommy Jenkins?"

"What are you doing here, Mrs. Miller?" From the way her Sig Sauer shook he was likely to shoot one of them accidentally. "You shouldn't be here."

His gaze dropped to the bed, his forehead wrinkling. "You guys had sex? Didn't you?" The gun steadied and returned to point at Chad. "Did you rape her? The way you did last time?"

"He's never raped me!" Lauren couldn't stop her response.

"Yes, he has. I saw it." Tom used both hands to steady his grip. The shaking stopped only marginally. "It was on all the websites, on all the news reports. He'd tied you up and blindfolded you. He made you," his voice dropped to a whisper, "do things. Bad things."

"Chad never raped me," she repeated, keeping her voice steady. How the hell could she get him to understand that she'd asked Chad to do that to her? That she enjoyed being bound and blindfolded. "He's never hurt me, Tommy. I promise."

"You're just saying that to protect him. You shouldn't do that. He's a bad man. You need to stay away from him. You hate him, remember? He killed your baby. He killed Emily."

"No. No, he didn't." She sidled away from Chad, attempting to draw Tom's attention away so Chad could get to the drawer where he'd stashed his gun. If they were lucky, Tom hadn't already found it.

She took another step toward him but also to the left, drawing his attention further away from Chad. "Chad didn't kill Emily. Neither of us did." She took a deep breath but didn't dare close her eyes the way she wanted. "She just stopped breathing. There was nothing either of us could have done."

"No! He killed her." With a roar of anger, Tom swung the gun back toward Chad, who dived to the floor at the same time the gun went off.

CHAPTER FIFTEEN

PAIN SEARED CHAD'S SHOULDER like someone had stabbed him with a red-hot poker. Even as he fell, Lauren kicked Tom in the back of the knees and grappled for the gun.

His right arm not working properly, Chad dragged himself across the floor, the six feet between him and his weapon a chasm wider than the Grand Canyon. Using his left hand, he opened the drawer and felt around inside until his fingers closed around the barrel of his Glock. He rolled over just in time to see Lauren's head snap back. Blood spurted across the room, splattering over the sheets. Lauren's body toppled sideways.

FUCK! Chad aimed his gun but Tom dragged Lauren to her feet and used her as a shield. "Stay back! I didn't want to hurt her but I had to. You saw—she was fighting me."

Lauren's head lolled onto her chest and he couldn't see her face properly, but from the blood trailing down her shirt, the bastard had probably broken her nose. Hopefully that's all he'd done. "Set her down, Tom. Please. Let me look after her. Let me make sure she's all right."

"Uh uh." Tom shifted Lauren's dead weight to one arm and lifted the gun, aiming it at Chad. He tilted his head until his mouth was less than an inch away from Lauren's ear, but his gaze never left Chad. "You shouldn't have come back, Mrs. Miller. You should have stayed away. He was miserable when you left. I was sad too but at least I knew you were safe."

Chad held his own gun steady but couldn't fire without risking Lauren's life. At least the gun was aimed at him, not at Lauren's head. Though the rest of Lauren didn't move, the fingers on Lauren's right hand made the "OK" sign. It was all he could do not to heave a sigh of relief. She was all right. If they kept their heads, if he could get control of this situation, they could still get out of this. Maybe. Tom still had that fucking gun.

Tom's eyes went unfocused, dreamy, his voice soft and distant. The arm holding the gun dropped a few inches but not enough. If Chad moved now, he'd still be gut-shot. "I loved you so much, Mrs. Miller. You were such a good mother to Emily."

"She was; you're right." Come on, Lauren, move. Drop to the floor. Something that'll get you out of the line of sight and give me a clean shot at him.

Tom's gaze cleared and the black barrel of the gun stared at Chad again. From this distance, a two fingered monkey couldn't miss hitting him. "Don't you talk to her. You're not good enough for her. That's why I had to keep her away from you. Keep her safe."

Chad held up the hand he could move, spreading his fingers wide. "All right. Let's just calm down."

"I kept her safe from you. I checked your mail box every day so you couldn't get any of the letters she sent you. I deleted all her messages from your answering machine. You didn't even know I was there. You thought you were so good with your security system. But you couldn't stop me."

Shit, he'd given Tom the security code and asked him to check his mail and water the plants when he was away. The whole time the little shit was the reason Lauren hadn't come home?

With a move so fast it startled even Chad who had been looking for a sign, Lauren dropped to the ground, taking Tom with her. As Tom swung around with a curse, aiming Lauren's own gun at her, Chad aimed and squeezed the trigger.

CHAPTER SIXTEEN

"THEY'VE CHARGED JENKINS with attempted murder and aggravated assault." Sam glanced at Lauren as she settled onto the arm of the couch beside Chad. "He's lawyered up, and isn't talking, but from what Andy's been able to find out through his sources his lawyers are seeking a psychiatric review while he's still in the hospital."

"They're looking for an insanity plea," Lauren surmised. "Or at least diminished capacity."

"They'll get it." Chad covered her knee with his left hand. His right was bound to his side, the bandage where they'd operated on the bullet not as thick as it had been the day before.

"What I don't get is why he waited this long to go after Chad."

"I'm guessing he saw the post on the web. It probably triggered something in him." The petite woman who Chad had introduced as Rosalinda Ramos, Sam's fiancée answered Lauren's question. "I talked to his mother. She said it's not the first breakdown he's had. That a couple of years ago he had a breakdown at school, enough that the counselors there suggested he come home for the semester. She thought it was the pressure at school, but now she wonders…"

"From there," Sam picked up where Rosie left off, "we're not sure if it was seeing you two together again that set him off. Or if he'd planned to go after Chad all along."

Lauren suppressed a smile. The duo were completing each other's sentences as if they'd been married for years.

"Almost forgot. Hey, Rosebud, you got those photocopies?"

Rosie reached into a voluminous purse and pulled out a manila file folder. "The police found these when they went through Tom's apartment. I got Andy to use his connections to make some copies since they have to keep the originals as evidence."

Lauren took the folder and handed it to Chad who placed it on his lap and opened it. Her breath caught in her throat when she recognized her own handwriting. "My letters."

After a glance at her, Sam nodded and returned his attention to Chad. "Looks like Tom had been going through your mail for years."

"I'd asked him to pick it up for me whenever I was travelling. I had no idea he'd been holding things back."

The room was silent except for the sound of rustling paper as Chad flipped through the letters. He stopped at the final one, written two years after she'd left. The one pleading with him to phone her, to give her some sign that he'd give her another chance.

He stared up at her, his heart in his eyes. "I'm sorry, babe. I would have replied if I'd known."

"It wasn't your fault." She covered his hand with hers and squeezed it. "But we've got a second chance now."

Sam stood, holding a hand out to help Rosie to her feet. "Well, Rosebud, I think that's our cue to leave these two alone."

Leaving Chad to rest on the couch, Lauren showed them to the front door. "Sam, I owe you an apology. I know I blamed you for Jill's death all these years. I was wrong. I'm sorry."

He quirked his eyebrows up. "I know. I'd say we both owe each other some apologies. I've been blaming you for walkin' out on Chad. I had no idea why you'd gone or what you were going through. If I'd known…" He nodded. "Yeah, we both had our demons to fight, didn't we?"

"So…are we friends again?"

"Yup." He grinned. "I heard you quit your other job. If you ever feel the itch to get back in the field, I know a good firm that's lookin' for people with your background."

"I may just take you up on that offer." Once she'd figured out the rest of her life.

"You do that." His grin faded and his gaze drifted to the room behind her. "It damned near killed him when you left. He stopped going home, started sleeping in the office for months at a time. I was afraid I was going to come in one day and find he'd eaten his gun."

"I didn't know. I thought…I got some bad intel and thought he'd remarried within a year."

"Mmm. Now I wonder where you heard that?" One dark eyebrow arched up, but when she didn't answer, Sam sighed. "Don't leave him again without telling him exactly why, you hear? Don't disappear the way you did last time. Or I'll come after you."

Without waiting for a reply, he headed for his car. Lauren stood in the doorway, until the Jag disappeared from sight.

Once she'd shut the door and rearmed the security system, Lauren returned to find Chad with his head against the back of the couch, his eyes closed. "You should go upstairs and have a nap."

He roused and smiled at her. The look he gave her was all heat. "You coming up with me?"

"Men! Even hurt and exhausted, all you can think about is sex." She folded her arms over her chest and tried not to smile. And failed.

"The problem with that is…?"

"As tempting as your offer is, if I lie down with you, you'll do anything but nap." She helped him to his feet and followed him upstairs.

Once they got to the bedroom, he started to undo his shirt left-handed. "Damn it, I'm all thumbs."

"Here, let me." She flicked open the buttons of his shirt, loving the familiarity of the task. Her smile dimmed when she caught sight of the bandage over his shoulder. It was smaller than the one the doctors had originally placed there, but it still looked obscene.

Chad rested his forehead on hers. "Hey, it'll heal, babe. I'll be fine."

"I could have lost you again," she whispered. "I shouldn't have left my gun out in plain sight. I should have locked it up so he couldn't get it."

"And I should have remembered to re-arm the security system so we would have had a warning. Hell, I should have locked the front door, but I had other things on my mind and I let myself get distracted." He stroked his thumb over her nipple until it beaded. "Stop blaming yourself. It's over. Harris is dead, and Tom's not a threat anymore either. We've got a second chance, babe. Let's not waste it."

"You're right."

"Of course I am. Now why don't you get undressed and join me? I'll let you be on top."

She had to laugh at the exaggerated leer he gave her. "You're incorrigible. All right, I'll lie down with you, but we're not going to do anything more than sleep."

She hovered over him while he took his pain pills and lay on the bed with him. Within five minutes, he was asleep and she found herself staring at the ceiling. Two weeks ago she'd only dreamt that she'd be lying here beside Chad again, and now her dreams had come true.

Yet there were still so many things unsettled between them.

CHAD ROLLED OVER, his arm instinctively seeking Lauren only to find...nothing. "Lauren?"

Had it all been a dream? He opened his eyes. The dent her head had left in the pillow was still there, the side of her bed messed. No, it hadn't been a dream. So why wasn't she still here?

Maybe she'd gone to the bathroom? Nope, the door was open and the light off. Where the hell had she gone?

His heart clogging his throat, he jogged downstairs, half afraid he'd find her bags missing. He pulled up short when he heard her talking in the kitchen.

"I meant what I said, Coop. I'm not coming back. I'm through with the Brigade."

Cooper was here? What the hell else did that bastard want? He'd already visited Chad at the hospital and threatened him until he'd signed a secrecy agreement similar to the one that bound Lauren.

"No, I haven't and I'm not going to either." There was a pause which told him that Cooper wasn't there in person, Lauren was talking to him on the phone. "No, you can't talk to him. He's sleeping...No, I am not waking him up so you can talk to him. He just got out of the hospital, damn it."

He was half-tempted to go into the kitchen and tell Cooper to go stuff himself, but he enjoyed hearing Lauren defend him. Other than Sam, he'd had precious few people in his corner. Besides, if he showed her he was awake, she'd probably insist on making him lunch—dinner, he revised having a glance at the chiming clock on the wall. He'd slept longer than he thought. While he was hungry, he preferred for her to come upstairs to wake him so he could make a meal of her.

He headed back to the stairs then saw the file folder containing the photocopies of Lauren's letters. Maybe he should read them before they made any long term decisions. He tucked the folder under his arm and headed back to the bedroom. Once he was stretched out on the bed, he steeled himself and opened the folder. From the looks of it, Sam had arranged the letters by the date they'd been sent.

April 26, 2002

Dear Chad,

I know you don't understand why I left without talking to you, but I was afraid of what I might do if I didn't get help right away. I've tried to be strong for you, but I just couldn't get my head clear. I've checked myself into a private hospital under an assumed name so the reporters can't attack you because of me...

The rest of the letter explained about Tranquil Pastures, and her diagnosis, just as she'd said. She'd pleaded with him to phone her or write her back.

May 11, 2002

130

...I love you, Chad. I'm so sorry for what I said during that fight. I know Emily didn't die because of anything you did. It was my fault, all mine, and I cannot beg your forgiveness enough...

The second letter continued, with yet another plea for him to write if he couldn't phone, to let her know he was all right, and asked if he'd consider visiting her until she was well enough to come home. So did the third. And the fourth.

The fifth letter wasn't written by Lauren but by her psychiatrist.

Dear Mr. Miller,

It is vital to your wife's recovery...

Chad crumpled the letter in his fist. Damn Tom Jenkins. Lauren had needed him.

Dear Chad,

He checked the date, this had been written six months after her first letter.

I've been praying that you'd get in contact with me after Dr. Maudsley wrote to you. Since we haven't heard from you, I can only assume you don't want me to come home to live with you when I'm released the day after tomorrow...

He closed his eyes. I would have come for you if I'd known, babe. Nothing could have stopped me.

February 13, 2004

Dear Chad,

I received the divorce papers from your attorney today. I had hoped that perhaps we could work on repairing our marriage, but Thalia tells me that you've been dating someone else for the past few months and that the two of you have moved in together. I hope she is stronger for you than I have been, and that she makes you happy because you deserve happiness. I will always regret that I couldn't be the one to give it to you.

I love you, and always will…

He had to read the last line twice, then re-read the first paragraph again. *Thalia* had told Lauren he was living with someone? Lauren had said once that she'd heard he was living with someone, but not once could he remember her saying that it was his own sister who had lied to her.

His phone rang. A quick check of the caller ID had him answering. "I was wondering how long it would take before you called, Coop."

"Lauren said you were asleep."

"I was." Yet you called me anyway. Arrogant ass.

Cooper grunted, which would be as close to an apology as he'd get Chad supposed. "I heard Sam came to visit you earlier."

"You heard or are you having us watched?"

"I ran into him and Rosie at the club, and he mentioned he'd dropped by. I thought I'd better make sure you completely understand that agreement you signed yesterday means you can't tell him anything about what you've learned."

Since I was still half doped up when you made me sign that fucking paper, you mean.

"I haven't said a word to him or anyone else." Yet. "And I want your assurance you will never use the club for anything related to the Brigade ever again. Because if I ever find you have put anyone at that club in danger, I am coming after you."

"Just make sure you keep your mouth shut to Sam. And anyone else."

"Considering you threatened to take me into custody if I didn't, I don't have much of a choice, do I? Are we done?"

"No. I want you to convince Lauren to come back and work for the Brigade. She doesn't have to go back into the field, but I need her."

Tough shit. So did he. So had he for nearly a decade. "That's not my decision to make, Coop. It's hers. If she wants to come back, I won't stand in her way, but if she doesn't, I'll support her a hundred and ten percent."

"Hmm, I'll remember you said that if you decide things won't work between you." Cooper's voice was cool, almost threatening.

"Whether we stay together or not, I'll still support her."

"Good to hear." To his surprise, Cooper sounded approving. "By the way, I know Lauren doesn't believe me but if I'd known what Thalia had done back then I would have told Thal to back off and made sure Lauren came home."

"Thalia? What the—" Cooper had already cut the connection and Chad found himself talking to no one.

Just what the fuck had Thalia done?

CHAPTER SEVENTEEN

LAUREN OPENED THE FRENCH DOORS and stepped onto the gray patio stones, the only ornament in the back garden. While Chad might have worked wonders inside the house, the yard had been left virtually untouched. In the spring, she'd plant daisies and black-eyed susans along the back fence. Maybe some sunflowers, and a rose trellis beside the patio so the fragrance could waft in when the door was open. And a fountain would be nice. One the birds could dart into and drink from or bathe in. There's always been something soothing about listening to trickling water in the lazy summer days.

If she still lived here next summer.

Chad had changed. So had she. Not for the worse. They were just…different. Subtle changes they'd both have to adjust to, accept. Yet so much about them was the same. He could still read her moods, still knew what she found exciting in the bedroom and knew the exact amount of force to set her on fire. But a marriage couldn't be built only on what happened in the bedroom.

The doorbell chimed, rousing her from her musings. After diverting to the kitchen to place her cup in the sink, she checked the monitor installed over the front door.

Thalia. Shit. She'd hoped it would be a couple more days before she'd face her again. Maybe she could just not answer the door. Pretend they weren't here.

After a gesture from her sister-in-law, Thalia's husband pressed the doorbell again. Damn it, they were going to wake Chad up if she didn't answer it.

Cursing under her breath, Lauren turned off the alarm and flipped the deadbolt. Steeling herself, she opened the door. "Hello, Thalia."

Thalia hissed and her eyes narrowed when she recognized who had opened the door. "What the hell are you doing here, Lauren? You're supposed to be in Europe."

"Nice to see you too. What do you want?"

"I heard that my brother had been shot. I came to see if he needed any help."

While Lauren couldn't fault Chad's sister for worrying about Chad, she resented the unspoken implication that she was incapable of caring for him. "He's fine. He may have to do some physio for a couple months, but he'll recover."

Ignoring her husband behind her, Thalia rolled her chair to the door. "I want to see him."

For the first time, Lauren realized the step had been designed as a ramp. As much as she wanted to leave Thalia on the doorstop and close the door between them, Chad would never appreciate her treating his sister that way. She sighed and opened the door all the way. "I really wish you'd come back another time. He's sleeping right now."

"Good." Thalia rounded on her. "I thought we had an agreement that you were to stay away from my brother. Permanently."

"You lied, Thalia. Repeatedly. That voided any agreement as far as I was concerned."

"You weren't right for him. I couldn't let you get back together so I did what I had to do to protect him."

"I love Chad, Thal. I always did, and I always will."

"You signed the divorce agreement quickly enough," Thalia sneered.

"Only because you told me he wanted to get married again. If I'd come back when I wanted to, we might have had a chance."

"He needed someone better than you. Someone stronger."

Lauren ran her hand through her hair. Eight years before, she'd have agreed. Now? Not a chance. "I trusted you, Thalia. I thought we were friends, but we weren't. Were we ever?"

"You were his wife—you were supposed to be on his side no matter what happened. You weren't there for him the way you should have been."

"I was there."

"No. You weren't. Not like me." Thalia rolled her chair forward, until Lauren was forced to step back. "You should have backed him a hundred percent for having the guts to go against orders to protect me. Instead you questioned him, argued with him about it. When that video got out, you should have held up your head and proudly admitted you submitted to him. That he was your Dominant. Yet you didn't."

She didn't bother correcting the whole Dominant thing. That was none of Thalia's business. But the video? She'd often wondered how the press had managed to get a video camera into their bedroom. "You did that, didn't you? You placed the camera in our bedroom."

"It had to be done."

"Why? Goddamn it, Thalia, why?" she shouted. "Why would you do that to us? Violate our privacy like that?"

"Because you didn't agree with Chad about his decision to protect me. To protect the club members. He saved my life with that decision, you selfish bitch," Thalia bit out. "If it had been up to you, I would have died. But all you could think about was your pitiful career."

"I understood why he felt he needed to protect you, but there were other ways to protect you. More official ways. I knew how much his career with the Bureau meant to him and he sacrificed it for you." Lauren's nails dug into her palms. "If he'd come to me, we could have found some other way to help protect the club. It was his not telling me what he'd done that was the issue between us. That's why I felt betrayed, because he didn't come to me first."

"He didn't tell you because you were too busy blaming him and everyone else for Emily's death," Thalia snapped. "It was your fault my niece died. Your fault."

"No, it wasn't."

They both looked to the top of the stairs where Chad stood, his good hand on the bannister, his gaze locked on Lauren. How much had he heard?

Thalia lifted her chin as Chad walked down the stairs to join them, but Lauren didn't miss the way her throat moved, the way the vein in her neck pulsed. Her sister-in-law was nervous.

"I heard about what happened. About the shooting." Thalia rolled her chair forward. "I can move in here and care for you. I can bring some of my people over to help out. You don't need her here."

"Is Lauren right? Are you the one who put that video camera in our bedroom?" Thalia looked away.

"You were, weren't you?" Chad's scowl deepened, his eyes grew dark as a thundercloud when he stopped in front of her. "Then you sent it to that goddamned gossip site who put it on the internet. Let it go viral."

"They had to see," she whispered. "You had to see her for what she was."

"What she was? She was my wife." He grabbed the armrest of her wheelchair and leaned until their noses were an inch apart. "You damned near irreparably damaged both of our reputations. You made it impossible for either of us to walk down the street without people making snide comments. If it hadn't been for Sam deciding to start Hauberk, I probably would have ended up a mall cop or asking a customer if they wanted fries with their order."

"I did what was necessary." Thalia's chin went down a half inch before she jerked it back up. "You need someone strong. Someone willing to get down on their knees and submit to you the way you deserved."

"That's your kink, not mine."

Lauren stifled her sigh when Thalia shook her head and persisted. "She's not good for you, Chad. Why am I the only one who can see that?"

"It's not your decision to make. It's mine." He moved to stand beside Lauren, slipped his arm around her waist. "I've asked Lauren to move back in with me. Whether we'll make it, I don't know yet, but hear me now: I will not tolerate any more interference. Because so help me God, Thal, if I find out you've been lying to me or withholding information or manipulating either of us ever again, I will cut you out of my life forever."

Chad glanced at Spencer. "Take your wife home and don't bring her back unless you personally hear me invite her."

He waited until the door had closed behind the couple before he spoke again. "I had no idea it had been Thalia who brought the divorce agreement to you, or that she'd told you I was marrying someone else."

"I know." Now.

"Why didn't you tell me it was Thalia? Were you afraid I'd believe her over you?"

"No. To be honest, that never occurred to me."

"So these past few days, why not say 'Thalia lied to me'? Why did you keep referring to her as 'someone' or 'I heard'? Why protect her after what she'd done to you? To us?"

Wasn't it obvious? "Because she's your sister. I didn't want to come between you."

"And you're my wife but that didn't stop her from coming between us." He wrapped his good arm around her and tucked her head beneath his chin. "Between Thalia with her lies and her videotape, and Jenkins stealing your letters…it's enough to make you wonder if they were conspiring to keep us apart."

She snuggled closer, enjoying being back in his embrace. Now that Thalia's manipulations had been brought into the light, the lingering guilt of not telling Chad dissipated. She felt like she could fly. Or burst into song. Neither of which would be pretty. "Paranoia, party of two, your table's ready."

"Even paranoids have enemies." Chad steered her to the stairs. "Think about it, Lauren. If Thalia hadn't taken that video of us, Tom may not have taken the letters trying to save you from me. If I'd read even one of those, I would have hopped on a plane and gone after you and—"

She pulled back and placed a finger over his lips. "Sssh. You can drive yourself crazy thinking like that. We can't change what's already happened or what others do as much as we wish we could. We can only control our own actions."

He touched his lips to her hair. "I know, but they kept me from the most precious thing in my life. I'm not sure I'll ever be able to forgive them for that."

"Give yourself time." They had all the time in the world now and she planned on not wasting another second.

Neither of them spoke when she took his hand and led him upstairs and into the bedroom. No words were needed as they undressed each other. Or when their lips touched. Or when he lowered her onto the bed, rolling beneath her, letting her take charge just the way he'd promised earlier.

Taking care not to touch his shoulder, Lauren stretched over his body and reclaimed his mouth. The outside world disappeared until only the two of them existed, filled with their languid explorations of each other, with gentle touches and soft sighs. Time slowed and stretched as if they'd never been apart.

When she could hold off no longer, Lauren positioned herself over Chad and bore down, taking him into her body an inch at a time. They both exhaled when their hips touched. His eyes dark, Chad caressed her breast, touching her reverently, carefully, as if she might shatter. She met his gaze, quickly losing herself within his deep gray depths.

The desire and passion of the very first time they'd made love flooded Lauren's soul. It twined itself around her heart and held fast.

With a light touch to her back, he drew her down until one nipple hovered above his mouth. When his lips closed over the sensitive bud, the sensation streaked through her and down to her pussy as if she'd been struck by lightning. His hands smoothed over her belly, following its path, his fingers finding her clit, pleasuring her until she could stay still no longer.

Whenever she started to speed up, he slowed her down. He stroked and suckled and teased until her whole body was quivering, heated until she was sure she would spontaneously combust. A simple touch of his thumb to her clit triggered an orgasm that shattered her into a thousand pieces of pure sensation.

When she finally could breathe, he started all over again, this time following her lead when her body clamped around him, milking his cock in the hardest orgasm she'd ever had.

Night had long since fallen before Chad finally spoke. "There's never been anyone else for me, Lauren."

He curled his fingers beneath her chin and turned her face until she looked at him. "I would have met you at the airport if I'd known you were waiting for my response. Hell, I should have flown to England to be with you as soon as I found out where you'd gone."

"You couldn't leave. Your inquiry was coming up."

"I didn't have to be there. They'd already made their judgment." He rested his forehead against hers.

"I loved you, Lauren. I would have done anything to get you back."

"Loved, past tense?" she whispered.

"No. Love. Past, present and future."

The fear and doubt Thalia had long ago planted withered. They could do this, they could make their marriage work. "I love you, too."

"Past, present and future?" His voice was hoarse and his thumb shook as he wiped the tears she hadn't realized had fallen.

Filled with hope that she hadn't had for years, she nodded. "I've never stopped loving you. I loved you then, I love you now. I'll love you forever."

Perfect Proposal

A Hauberk Protection story

BY LEAH BRAEMEL

This is a follow up to Sam and Rosie's story in *Personal Protection*, but takes place just after *Deliberate Deceptions* and during *Hidden Heat's* timeframe but doesn't give any spoilers. If you haven't read *Personal Protection* yet, you probably should

Sometimes the best laid plans go every way but the way you want…

Sam Watson wants to propose to the love of his life, Rosie Ramos, but all his previous attempts have been thwarted. Every. Single. Time. This time he's determined that nothing, and no one, will get in his way. No interruptions. No exceptions. Not from work, not by family busybodies, not even if the roses crucial to his plans are lost. Nothing will stop him.

If only someone had let Rosie in on his plans…

Warning: Contains misguided intentions, a hunky hero with more than just a ring burning a hole in his pocket, and a spitfire girlfriend who counters with her own proposal. The romance may be sweet but the sex is explicitly hot, hot, hot.

Perfect Proposal

A Hauberk Protection story

LEAH BRAEMEL

DEDICATION

For Laura N, aka Mrs. Sam Watson, may your father be with you every time you makes his *Churrasco con chimichurri*

CHAPTER ONE

SUNLIGHT GLINTED OFF THE SOLITAIRE diamond engagement ring and fractured into a thousand rainbows that danced over the walls and ceiling. Heedless of the display, Sam Watson juggled the hotel phone between his ear and shoulder. "What do you mean, the roses haven't arrived? I ordered them last month."

"We're looking into the situation now, Mr. Watson," the concierge responded. "We're working with the florist to locate them and they'll be in your room by the time you return tonight."

Sam pinched the bridge of his nose, mentally running through his checklist. What else could go wrong? "You understand I want everything to be perfect tonight, right? It's not just about the roses. I want the champagne chilling in the ice bucket, the music cued up, candles ready to be lit. It's gotta be perfect, you hear me?"

Unlike the last three times he'd planned to propose, only to have his plans go awry. Rosie deserved perfect and if it killed him, he'd give her the perfect memory. The perfect proposal.

"Yes, sir. I'll personally ensure everything is exactly as you've requested, even if I have to go out and purchase the roses myself."

"Make sure they're red roses. Not pink. Not white. Red." To match his favorite shade of her lipstick.

"Yes, sir. All I need from you now is an approximate time you'll be returning so we can be set up and out of your way."

Now there was a problem. Every member of the Ramos family could talk the ears off a concrete elephant. A regular dinner generally lasted two hours—a birthday dinner might last until dawn. The way his luck was running lately, he hedged his bet. "Set it up before six." Dinner shouldn't be cooked and eaten before then, he doubted. "That way we won't walk in on your staff and ruin the surprise. And call me if you can't get the damned roses."

After another assurance from the concierge that all would be done according to plan, he hung up the phone. Good thing too, because at some point during the call the shower had shut off. He closed the small blue box and slipped it back into his coat pocket moments before Rosie emerged. As it did every time she walked into a room, his whole body went on alert, needing to claim her.

A drop of water slid from the tip of one dark curl and over the curve of her breast before disappearing into the towel she'd tucked into her cleavage. Damned lucky towel.

Some of their clients had thought her natural sensuality, along with petite stature, made her less effective as a bodyguard. At least until he explained that those qualities made her less likely to scare the bejesus out of a client's kids or pass undetected by anyone expecting to see a six-foot-six behemoth like himself. After that, he'd have Rosie give them a demonstration by taking him down with a quick-and-dirty leg sweep, or show them the results of her last shooting competition.

A second, then a third droplet followed the path of the first. He skimmed a finger over her skin, tracing the path the water droplets had taken to the edge of the towel.

"Well, were you?"

"Was I what?" Was the towel slipping? If it wasn't, it should. A slight tug should be enough to—

The single finger tilting his chin until he met her eyes made him focus, as did the impatient tapping of her tiny foot. "Saa-am…"

Uh-oh, she was getting that tone in her voice. She'd said something, but damned if he knew what. "Sorry. I got distracted. What did you ask?"

She clamped a hand across her bosom, which only served to press the soft mounds until a hint of cinnamon nipple peeked over the terry. With her free hand she made a V with her fingers and aimed them at her face in an unspoken "eyes up here, buddy" command.

After a brief internal struggle he managed to wrench his gaze back to her face. Her narrowed eyes told him she knew exactly what had distracted him.

"I asked—"she enunciated every syllable, drawing his gaze to her lips, still swollen from their earlier kisses, "—if you were talking to me while I was in the shower."

Shoot, he'd figured between her singing and the running water she wouldn't hear him talking. "Nope. I was—"Keep your eyes up, Watson, stop thinking about getting her naked, "—checking in with Chad."

"I know it's a blow to your ego, but Chad doesn't need you to micromanage things. He's perfectly capable of running the office himself. And you took a couple of days off to relax." She poked her index finger into the middle of his chest. "So relax already."

"Hey, he contacted me first." He didn't have to mention that his second-in-command had reached him by text message, which is how he'd replied. "It's not my fault the guy's OCD about details." Which was what made Chad so good at his job.

Her expression softened. "I worry about you, Sam. You've been working so hard lately. You deserve this vacation. Chad can handle any issues that come up back in D.C."

"I know, but—"

"No buts. Now promise me you won't be checking your email or texting him all day. Give yourself some time for fun."

The scent of her shampoo—a light fragrance of ginger and some other spice—filled his lungs. Damn, she smelled good enough to eat. A quick check over his shoulder at the hotel room clock showed he had time to do a little taste test of the smorgasbord known as Rosalinda Ramos. Taste test, hell! Count him in for a whole sit-down dinner with her laid out as the main meal. He gave in to temptation and tugged at the terry tucked into her cleavage. "Well, lookie here, your towel's come loose."

Damned if she didn't thwart him by pressing her whole body against him to hold it in place. "I know I said you should have fun but we're due at my parents' in less than an hour. We don't have time for sex right now."

He raised his eyebrows and drew himself up to his full six foot six to stare down at her. "There's always time for sex."

She slapped at his chest with little heat. "I still have to dry my hair—"

With her tight curls, drying meant using a boatload of hair products to help keep her hair straight and tame, which took her at least forty-five minutes.

"—and do my make-up."

Shoot, he could have waited an hour or more to get dressed up in this monkey suit. At least he could loosen his tie while he waited. And maybe his fly. He always got a hard-on watching her apply her makeup—especially her lipstick, while he imagined the particular shade on her lips as they closed around his cock the way they had earlier.

"Then I have to get dressed." The conviction in her voice faded as she nuzzled her face against his chest.

Yeah, they were definitely going to be late, thanks to the erection painfully constrained by his briefs.

"We can blame traffic if we're late." He slipped his hands beneath the terrycloth and palmed her bare ass. Drowning in Rosie's sensuality, he gave in and allowed his carnal side to take over.

Rosie gasped when he lifted her until they were nose-to-nose, her feet dangling a foot off the floor. Though she teased him about lugging her around like she was a suitcase, she found his penchant for picking her up as though she weighed nothing incredibly romantic.

With a shake of her head in mock dismay, she locked her hands around his neck and hooked her legs around his hips. "You're incorrigible, you *payaso*."

"Even a clown would get hard watching you parade around in nothin' but a towel, Rosebud." As proof of the truth of his statement, he pressed his erect cloth-covered shaft against her mound.

She should have anticipated this when he'd ogled her cleavage instead of listening to her. Oh heck, she'd seen the look he'd given her when she'd headed into the shower, and quite frankly she'd been surprised he hadn't joined her. The fact that they'd already made love before breakfast never slowed Sam Watson down.

"Have I told you I love you this morning?" he asked.

He had. Numerous times, in English, Spanish, French and what she thought might be German—once he'd discovered she got turned on by foreign languages, he'd exploited her weakness without a qualm.

"I love you too." She nipped at his earlobe and sighed, just as disappointed as she was about to make him. She lowered her legs to the floor, leaving her arms around his neck, forcing him to bend over. "I have to get dressed."

"No, you need to stay naked." His gaze dropped again, lingered. A smile played at the corners of his lips. "Drop the towel and get on your knees, Princesa."

He didn't really want her to go down on him now, did he? Then again, they'd set the rules right at the outset of their relationship that he would never call her Princesa outside of a scene. His use of it now meant he was serious.

"We don't have time, Sam." She eyed him suspiciously. "I told Mama I'd be there to help her. I don't want to be late—you realize she'll know what we've been doing."

"We've got time." He tugged on the hem of the towel. "Drop the towel, Princesa. Now."

A second use of her nickname. While she enjoyed pushing his boundaries, this wasn't the time. Without another thought, she released the towel and lowered herself to her knees in front of him. Her nipples beaded tight in the cool air after the warmth of the shower, but the rest of her body heated.

What was it about her that loved when he let his dominant side come out to play? She carried a gun and as one of Hauberk's lead operatives, other people obeyed her orders. So why were her breasts aching for his touch, her pussy rippling in anticipation of dropping to her knees in front of him?

He unzipped his pants and freed his cock, long and hard, from his trousers. She reached up to touch him, but he stopped her. "Lace your fingers together behind your back."

She leaned forward and let the fat head of his cock slip over her lips, her tongue darting out to lick the salty bead at the slit. He groaned and fisted his hands in her hair, holding her in place to thrust his shaft past her lips and over her tongue.

Since she couldn't move, or touch him with her hands, she sucked hard on his head, her tongue lashing the sensitive spot at its rim. His grunts rumbled through the room as she swallowed him until her nose brushed the dark wool of his suit and the head of his cock bumped the back of her throat. Letting her teeth scrape his length, she pulled back. Alternating the suction, she repeated the process, loving the bite of pain from his hold on her hair.

His hips flexed, pumping faster, his eyes unfocused and his face screwed up tight as if he were in pain, a sign he was close to losing control. Was there anything better than knowing she had such power over him?

With a snarl, Sam loosened his grip and pulled from her mouth. "Turn around. Brace your arms on the desk."

Damn, she'd wanted to watch him when he came. She did as he ordered and parted her legs to give him easier access. Thank heavens for the mirror over the desk; she could still watch him.

His Savile Row suit scratched her ass, reminding her he was still dressed while she was completely naked. The white of his crisply starched shirt accentuated the perpetual tan of his Hawaiian heritage. At her urging, he'd let his hair grow longer. Soon it would be a shock of thick waves she had to pay a fortune to her stylist to achieve.

He smiled back at her, traced the Blue Morpho butterfly tattoo at the base of her spine. "You think I don't realize you like to watch too?"

She couldn't stop her snort of derision, despite appreciating that he'd indulged her voyeuristic side. "Yeah, I love looking at myself when my hair looks like Medusa's."

There was no mistaking the love in his eyes, but his lips firmed and he shook his head. "I love the untamed look."

An I'm-gonna-ride-you-hard promise strong in his eyes, Sam wrapped a strand of her hair around one finger and tugged hard enough to create the little zip of pain she loved. "Stop arguing with me. You're beautiful, and that's the end of it."

Her pussy got even wetter when he unwound her hair from his finger and caressed her ass. His gaze captured hers in the mirror when he slipped one hand between her parted thighs. Satisfaction flared in his expression.

"Yeah, you're already drippin' wet. I'm not the only one who gets off when you're sucking on my cock, am I?"

Two fingers thrust into her pussy while another taunted her clit. A shudder rolled through her, and she writhed her hips to increase the pressure. With a frown, Sam delivered a stinging slap on first one butt cheek then the other with his free hand. "Stay still."

Oh crap, the sting changed to warmth that made her pussy pulse harder.

Without warning, his hands left her. The bed creaked when he sat, reached into the bedside table and withdrew a condom.

"I could help you." Remembering the last time she'd helped him, she couldn't stop her smile. He'd taken her with a ferocity that had left her aching two days later. Hmm, maybe if she wanted to get out of here faster... No, there were some things worth savoring. Heaven knew Sam loved to savor.

"Nope, I've got it." Seconds later, he met her gaze in the mirror once more. His shirt was still buttoned up, his silk tie in place, but his pants were now on the floor beside her towel. He held out his hand; the second her fingers touched his, he pulled her between his thighs. "Climb up on me, but stay facing the mirror."

Following his directions, she straddled his legs and leaned her back against his chest. His arm banded around her waist, holding her in place, one large hand palming her breast. He lowered her onto his shaft in one thrust.

"Don't close your eyes," he whispered, his voice dark and edgy. "Keep looking in the mirror."

It wasn't the warmth of his breath that sent shivers down to her toes and back up again. The image of them, her hair wild and tousled, his curls dark and neat, the tanned skin of his wrist against the white of hers, his large palm cupping her breast, was one of the sexiest sights she'd witnessed. But none of it matched his expression of sheer carnality.

"I love watching you come." He fondled her nipples between his thumb and forefingers. Heat zipped from his fingers to her pussy. "I love knowing you come only for me."

As she watched, his large hand slid over the soft skin of her belly to the apex of her thighs. His fingers parted her glistening folds, allowing a full view of his cock buried deep within her. The sight nearly caused her to orgasm. He found the hard nub of her clitoris and circled it slowly, teasing her until the scent of her arousal—and his—filled the air.

"Now ride me. Hard and fast."

With pleasure. Flattening her palms on his thighs, she lifted herself, loving how his shaft caressed her. When she'd lifted as far as she dared, she rotated her hips to tease him then reversed course, squeezing her pussy around his cock until they both groaned.

"Enough of this teasing," he growled. His arm tightened in an iron grip as he pumped deep inside her, his fingers flicking in rhythm against her clitoris, setting a flame that raced through the rest of her body.

Before she could control it, her climax consumed her, drowning her. She lifted her eyes to see him watching in the mirror, pride and lust clear in his eyes.

"My turn." Somehow he managed to stand, still holding onto her with his cock buried deep inside. He laid her face-down on the desk, the wood cool on her breasts, and lifted her hips slightly. "Hang on. I'm not going to be gentle."

He was true to his word, and she loved every thrust and plunge deep within her. His balls slapped against her clit with every press forward until her pussy quivered around his hard shaft. His fingers dug into her thighs, canting her hips at a slightly different angle.

The desk bumped against the wall in time with his thrusts. Some distant part of her brain wondered if there was anyone in the adjoining room listening. Who cares? she thought muzzily. They were in one of the swankiest rooms in New York City and she was with the man she loved. A man who loved her. Who cared who heard them?

Any concern over the noise they made disappeared when his hand snaked between them once more and flicked the swollen bundle of nerves, driving her past the edge of control. A half dozen thrusts later, Sam stiffened behind her, his cock jerking against her sensitized flesh, stimulating yet another orgasm of her own.

After a groan, he kissed her shoulder and pulled his softening cock from her body. "That should hold me off until tonight."

Rosie straightened, wobbling slightly, and sank back on the bed. "Where do you get the energy? Most men wouldn't be able to get it up again for a week after this morning's exercises."

"Exercises?" His dark brows drew together. "I don't consider making love to you an exercise." He braced his arms on either side of her head and captured her mouth, tasting of coffee and Sam. "It's a privilege to make you come, Rosie."

"You say the nicest things." She flattened her hand against his chest with more than a little regret. "But I have to get dressed. Or you'll be the one to apologize to my mother for making us late."

"Your mother likes me too much to get mad." He fondled her breast as if considering continuing their play, then let his hand fall. "Go get dressed, but I'll still claim a rain check for when we get back tonight."

To Sam, a rain check meant an entire weekend at his command, which usually meant they never left the bedroom, whether at home or at his private club. Ha! He'd hear no argument from her.

CHAPTER TWO

BY THE TIME THEIR TAXI STOPPED in front of her parents' home in the Bronx, every inch of her skin tingled as if he'd touched everywhere with his fingers instead of his gaze. The places he had touched her—the small of her back when escorting her from their room to the lobby, the sensitive skin by her ear when he'd toyed with her hair earlier, the inside of her wrist, where even now his thumb stroked while he held her hand—ramped up the need until her insides threatened to spontaneously combust.

The moment the limo stopped in front of her parents' house, the front door opened. Teresa Ramos hurried down the porch steps to meet them, the fat snowflakes liberally coating her dark hair.

Without waiting for the driver to round the car, Rosie flung open the door, dashed up the sidewalk and hugged her mother. "Mama, you should put a coat on. It's chilly. You'll catch a cold."

"Oh, I'm fine. And how many times did I have to tell you to put a coat on when you were little, huh?" Her mother gave her one last hug. "You look happy, *Cariño*. But tired, I think."

"I am happy, Mama."

At that pronouncement, her mother beamed and turned to Sam. "How are you, *Oso*? Thank you for bringing my Rosie home for my birthday."

Grinning at the nickname her mother had given him the first time they'd met, Sam leaned down to engulf the tiny woman in a hug. "I'm good, Mama Ramos. And nothing would have kept Rosie from her family."

"Ah, what are we doing standing out here on the street? Come inside. Everyone's waiting for you. I left Emilio's newest girlfriend to slice the plantains for the *platanutres*." Mrs. Ramos shook her head and tsked. "I don't know about this girl—I hope he's not serious about her."

They'd scarcely made it through the front door before her family swarmed around her, each member intent on imparting the latest news in the Ramos household. Her two-month-old niece, Isabel, found her way into Rosie's arms while Isabel's older brother, Rafael, with his thumb stuck firmly in his mouth, eyed them suspiciously. Greetings and the latest updates in the plans for dinner and shopping the next day whirled around her in a miasma of sound.

By the time she'd managed to hand Isabel back to her sister-in-law, Rosie found her eldest brother, Jose, at the near end of the couch, his son in his lap, occupied by one of their inevitable football discussions with their younger brother, Emilio. At the far end of the couch, Sam responded in fluent Spanish to her father's discussion of the latest trouble down at his precinct.

"He fits right in, doesn't he?" Jose's wife, Elba, whispered.

He did.

"Stop admiring your men, you two." Mrs. Ramos poked Rosie in the shoulder. "Come help me in the kitchen."

***

SAM PULLED HIS ATTENTION AWAY from the pregame show when Rosie's younger brother handed him a beer.

Emilio cracked open his beer and sank into a chair opposite, one leg hooked over the arm. "Hey Sam, are you in a Fantasy Football league? Because you should consider taking our quarterback for your team."

"Yeah, if you want Sam to lose, he should take your quarterback." Jose waved a hand over his son and shifted his sleeping boy in his arms. "Aw, Jeez Louise, Raph, why couldn't you wait to crap your pants until your momma was around?"

"What the hell have you been feeding that boy?" Holding his hand over his nose, Emilio leaned as far away from his nephew as he could. "So, Sam, Giants or Jets?"

Sam considered arguing for his beloved Redskins before deciding he needed all the points he could get with the Ramos family. Especially when he approached her father to ask for permission to marry Rosie. Sure, most guys didn't bother with such formalities these days, and the Ramos' didn't seem a particularly old-fashioned couple, but it never hurt to get on a future in-law's good side. Not to mention that if he and Rosie ever had a daughter, he'd definitely want a say in who she'd marry. When the hell had he gotten so old-fashioned?

He was still mulling over the question when Mr. Ramos stood up with a groan. "I'm going out for a smoke."

A chance to get him alone? Sam was all over that opportunity. "I'll join you, Carlos."

Mr. Ramos' eyebrows merged. "I thought Rosalinda made you give up smoking your cigars?"

"She did." Rather than taking the chance at being put off, Sam stood and headed for the door. "I need some fresh air."

Behind him, Emilio snorted. "Hey, blame Jose. He's the one who is too lazy to get up off his ass and change his kids' diaper."

"He's sleeping," Jose argued. "Do you have any idea how hard it is to get him to sleep? Fricking hard. Which means I'm not about to wake him up. When you have kids, you'll put up with a little stink for a moment's peace too."

Okay, so that was another reason to get out of the room—for a cute kid, Raphael was definitely ripe. Yet watching the kid asleep on his father's chest had sent unfamiliar pangs through Sam's gut. What would it be like to have his own son—or daughter—in his arms like that one day? Was it fair to bring a child into this uncertain world?

He was still wondering about fatherhood when Mr. Ramos and he were halfway down the block. The drizzle that had been falling when they'd arrived changed to fat flakes, and the wind had picked up, making Sam grateful that he'd accepted Rosie's advice to bring his leather coat.

His nicotine fix achieved, Mr. Ramos stopped in the middle of the sidewalk and took another drag on his cigarette. "What's on your mind, son?" He lifted his chin and exhaled a plume of smoke, watching it swirl and dissipate in the chill air. "Don't pretend you came out here for the fresh air. You want to talk to me about something."

Ah. Figured he couldn't pull anything over on Rosie's dad. He removed the ring box from his coat pocket and opened it, revealing the ring. "I want to propose to Rosie later tonight but I thought I should ask you first." Fingers crossed she'd say yes this time.

"That's quite the rock." Mr. Ramos scowled at the end of his cigarette for a moment. "My daughter doesn't need our permission to marry you—we raised her to know her own mind. She'll do what she wants."

"I thought—"

"You thought you'd win a few points with her mother and me by the gesture." Mr. Ramos lifted his cigarette and took another drag, holding the smoke in his lungs for a second before exhaling. "The only question is, does my Rosalinda want to marry you?"

Now there was the question. He'd asked her before and been turned down flat. While he'd understood her concerns about how short a time they'd been together at that stage, and how haunted he'd been about his previous girlfriend, he'd shut up on the subject, figured time would prove he was with her for the long haul. Only thing he'd not figured out was how long he should wait to ask a second time without spooking her. So he figured he'd wait for her to mention something first. Drop some hints about making things permanent, but she hadn't. At least none that he could discern.

"You're hesitating." Mr. Ramos' eyebrows stretched into his hairline. "You aren't sure if Rosie loves you? Because anyone with eyes can see she does. Or is there trouble in paradise?"

"I know she loves me." Of that, he had no doubt. "As much as I love her."

So why had the butterflies that had niggled in his stomach gained ten pounds? Because, dumbass, you're afraid she'll say no a second time.

"I'm glad to hear that." Another drag, another puff. "But if she says no, you will not take it out on her. You will not make her job difficult or make her unhappy. Or I will come visit you." He flicked his butt to the curb, and a smile that reminded Sam of Dr. Seuss' Grinch crept across Ramos' face. "Or worse, my wife will."

CHAPTER THREE

ROSIE SNITCHED A CRACKER from the plate Elba was putting together and, like her sister-in-law, layered on a slice of *salchichon*, a smear of guava paste and a slice of the cheese, topping it with an olive. Unlike Elba who faithfully placed another cracker creation on the plate, Rosie took a bite of hers. The combination of cheddar and dried sausage had her moaning in delight.

Mrs. Ramos slid a pan of pork pasteles into the oven to stay warm. "Mrs. Santos is retiring next month and then she's moving to Florida, can you believe it? I've bought pasteles from her for twenty years and all of a sudden she just up and leaves. Now I have to find someone new to buy them from."

"Why don't you make your own?" Noelle, Emilio's flavor of the month, nibbled at the edge of a piece of the sausage before discarding it with a scowl.

Rosie ducked her head to hide her smile, although she'd tasted her mother's pasteles the time her mother and Mrs. Santiago had had words and her mother had declared she could make them herself. The whole family had quickly dissuaded her of that notion. Every year since, the whole family ensured the freezer was filled with Mrs. Santiago's pasteles so they wouldn't have to endure any more of their mother's attempts.

"No one I know makes their own." Elba switched from the crackers to piling the deep fried plantain chips onto a serving dish and handed them to Rosie's mother. "There's always some lady in the neighborhood who we buy them from and then we stick them in the freezer for when we need them."

"I hate cooking." Noelle snagged one of the chips as Mrs. Ramos walked past. "Hey, these are good. Anyway, when I get married, I'm going to make sure the guy has enough money that we can eat out every night. Or if I'm really lucky, we'll be able to afford to hire someone to cook for us."

Rosie exchanged a glance with Elba, who shook her head and shrugged that screamed the same "where had Emilio dug this one up?" frustration Rosie was feeling.

"I like to cook," Rosie said, "especially when Sam helps me." She could feel the color rise in her face at the memory of her attempt to make tembleque. Sam had come in to help her but decided she made a tastier dessert than her coconut pudding. By the time they'd finished, the milk and the rest of the ingredients she'd set on the stove to heat had long since scalded. They'd ended up tossing the whole thing, even the saucepan in the trash. Good thing her mother wasn't in the room—she would have questioned Rosie's blush. There were very few things she couldn't discuss with her mother, but her sex life with Sam and all that entailed was at the top of the list.

Noelle hitched her hip on the counter. "You're so lucky to have found a sugar daddy who's under the age of fifty. And he's so freaking drool-worthy too."

"He's not my sugar daddy."

This again? It had bothered her initially that many of Sam's friends thought she was with him only for his money. Oh, he was handsome enough, but people usually found his most attractive feature the size of his bank account.

The eye roll Noelle gave her could have been seen by balcony patrons of any Broadway theater. "Don't give me that. His watch alone has to have cost at least five K. And that suit must have set him back a thousand, easy. Anyone with eyes can tell it's not off the rack. Not to mention he brought you here in a limo when the rest of us have to take the subway or regular cabs. The man's loaded. You hit the jackpot with him. You'll never have to work again if you don't' want to. Do you know how many women would jump all over him?"

She did. Too many women hit on him, even with her watching. Sam shrugged them off, but he couldn't stop the catty comments when they encountered her privately.

"Not that it's any of your business, but I love Sam for who he is, not what he has. I'd be with him if he was a security guard at Walmart."

"If you say so." Noelle curled her lip, then straightened and jumped off the counter when Rosalinda's mother returned. "It's not like he's asked you to marry him or anything. Which, girlfriend, should tell you something about the future of your relationship. How long have you been together now?"

"For your information, he has proposed." Ay. Why had that confession popped out? Rosie picked up the plate of crackers, intent on taking them to the guys.

Rosie's mother's whole face lit up. "Rosalinda! He's already asked you? Why didn't you tell me?"

She fended off her mother's immediate hug. "Because we're not engaged, mama. He proposed after we'd only been together for a couple of months. I wasn't sure about a few things back then." Like whether he was over his dead girlfriend. "So I said no." Something she'd regretted shortly after, but didn't know how to approach him about, so she'd waited for him to ask again. And waited.

Noelle snorted. "Big mistake."

Mrs. Ramos pried the plate from Rosie and shoved it in Noelle's direction. "Why don't you take these out to the men, dear? And while you're out there, get Carlos and Emilio to bring in the extra chairs for the dining room. With you, Sam and Rosie, we'll need three more."

Once Noelle wandered out of the kitchen, Rosie's mother sighed. "I hope Emilio isn't serious about that girl. I'd have a word with him, but it would probably drive him to her even faster. That boy always has been contrary." She gave Rosie a concerned look. "Now about you and your Oso. If you weren't ready to say yes, then you were right to wait to make sure he's the right man for you."

"He is the right man for me, mama."

She opened the fridge and removed the octopus salad to hand to Elba before facing Rosie again. "I'm not saying this to pressure you, but you've been together long enough to have some sort of commitment. I know many people don't feel it's necessary to get married these days, but what's the harm with making it official?"

"It's not that I'm against marriage, mama—"

"He loves you, Rosalinda. This I can see with my own two eyes. And you love him. Why not get married?"

"Because he hasn't asked again. I've tried to bring it up since but he doesn't seem to get the hint." As a former FBI agent, Sam caught onto nuances and subtleties faster than she did, but when it came to marriage, he was like most other guys she'd met. Clueless. "Besides, it's just a piece of paper."

A calculating gleam appeared in her mother's expression. "The timing is perfect. We could wander through the bridal gown section at Saks tomorrow. Get you registered for gifts."

"Mama, he hasn't asked, remember? We're not engaged yet."

"Why don't you ask him outright?" Elba suggested. "These days, there's nothing saying the man has to be the one to ask. Find out where you stand before you put much more time into this relationship."

Rosie slipped from the kitchen and found Sam sprawled on one end of the couch, listening to a discussion between her brothers about the newest Jets quarterback. Why hadn't she asked Sam outright about marriage before this? She'd never been one to wait for others to decide her fate, and heaven knew subtlety usually wasn't her style.

The moment he saw her, Sam shot that brilliant bright smile that had her knees weakening. "Hey, Rosebud, come join us. Emilio here doesn't think your Jets or my Redskins have a shot at the Superbowl this year."

"I wouldn't put much stock in his arguments from a Giants' fan." She took his hand and let herself be drawn onto his lap, only to draw back with a frown. "You're cold. What've you been doing?"

"I went out for a little walk, that's all. You done in the kitchen?"

After a moment's consideration, she nodded. Dinner was almost ready, and there were already too many cooks in the kitchen. They could do without her for a few minutes more.

"Good. I've missed you." He settled her head under his chin. "Hey, Carlos, who are you bettin' on for next week's game?"

Content to be a spectator to the discussion rather than a part of it for once, Rosie snuggled even deeper against Sam's chest. The combination of the lingering scents of the shaving cream with his subtle aftershave and the starch of his shirt wound through her head.

He'd discarded his jacket, loosened his tie and undone the top button of his shirt. In her opinion, there was nothing as sexy as that tiny peek at his chest, letting her imagination provide the rest of the image. Beneath her palm, she could feel the bump of the stellate scar, where a bullet had nearly ended his life. If she skimmed her hand to the center, she'd feel the long scar left when they'd cracked open his chest. She could have lost him before she'd even met him. Her insides clenched and she squeezed her eyes shut at that thought.

Noelle's question gnawed its way into her brain. If he wanted something badly enough, Sam wasn't the type of guy to take no for an answer. So why hadn't he proposed again? Questions that had assailed her late at night, long after Sam had fallen asleep, flooded her again. Had she insulted him by turning him down that first time? Did he think she wouldn't respond differently next time? Or had he realized he didn't want to marry her after all? Why hadn't she said something and asked him herself?

Elba was right. She should take the bull by the horns, or the Oso by his lapels. Just not here in front of her family.

He nuzzled her hair and whispered, "What's up?"

Was she that transparent? "Nothing."

"You may be selling, but I ain't buyin' it. You sighed in that way you do when something's gnawing at you, so don't shine me on about nothin' bein' wrong."

Before Rosie could respond, her mother called from the dining room "Carlos, Jose, Emilio, didn't Noelle tell you to bring more chairs in here? Dinner's ready and there aren't enough seats for everyone."

To Rosie's relief, the topic got lost amongst the bustle of the men bringing in the chairs, then everyone choosing a place at the table and helping themself to the food. During the dinner, Sam good-naturedly bore the brunt of her brothers' attempts to fool him about what the various dishes contained.

At the end of the meal, Raphael climbed out of his booster seat and toddled over to Sam. The youngster held his hands in the air in front of Sam. "Up."

"Hey there, buddy." Rosie's breath stuttered when Sam settled the boy on his lap "You want to share my rice pudding?"

Her nephew nodded and reached for the spoon, spilling half the contents of the arozzo con dulce over Sam's brand new suit.

Elba jumped to grab her son, but Sam waved her off. "Don't worry about it. We're good here." He took control of the spoon, refilled it with more pudding and lifted it to Raphael's lips. "There ya go, buddy."

Rosie's mother nudged her beneath the table. Once she had Rosie's attention, she leaned over and whispered, "Elba's right. If he won't ask you, you should ask him." With that pronouncement, her mother stood and started gathering the dishes.

"Mama, sit down. It's your birthday. We're doing the dishes tonight." She stared pointedly at her brothers, who groaned. "All of us, not just Elba and I."

Rosie stayed quiet while she and her siblings washed the dishes and dealt with the leftovers. Once everything had been stored away, she wandered out to the living room and curled up beside Sam, letting her family's chatter flow around her once again.

While her mother opened her presents, Sam pressed a kiss to her hair. "You're quiet again. Now 'fess up, what's going on in that head of yours?"

"I ate too much, that's all." She pressed one hand against her too-fully belly. It wasn't a lie. She was going to have to add a couple of miles to her run for the next week or three. "And I'm tired. Someone woke me up early this morning."

"Why don't you take my daughter back to the hotel for a nap?" Rosie's father suggested, one thick eyebrow twitching. What was wrong with him? "She'll need her energy if she's to go shopping with her mother and Elba tomorrow."

Sam shifted and pulled her closer. "You want to go back to the hotel, Rosie?"

With a faked yawn, she nodded. "Yeah, I think we should. I'll see you in the morning, Mama."

Her mother looked startled when both Rosie and Sam stood, but she nodded. "Let me get you some leftovers in case you get hungry later tonight."

Despite Rosie's protests that she wouldn't be hungry for a week, her mother pressed a plastic bag containing several reusable containers into Sam's hands. "You take these. I also know that a big fellow like you will be looking for a snack soon, and hotel food is too expensive to be charging all the time. And thank you for bringing my daughter home for my birthday."

"You're welcome, Mama Ramos."

"You bring her back for her birthday, too." Her father called from his chair. "I always makes her *Churrasco con chimichurri* for her."

"It's a Brazilian skirt steak," Rosie explained, "made with olive oil, garlic—"

"Now don't start giving away my secret recipe," Carlos objected. "S*olo para tiiiiiii.....no paraaaa todaaaa la gente.*"

"All right, I'll keep your secrets." Rosie kissed her father's cheek. "But you don't need to worry. No one makes it as good as you, Papa."

"If you bring your fellow back, maybe," Mr. Ramos eyed Sam, "just maybe, I'll teach him how to make it for you too."

"I'd like that, Carlos. But for now, I need to get Rosie back to the hotel." Sam bent down and bussed a kiss across Mrs. Ramos' cheek, shook her father's hand and climbed into the limo after Rosie.

Once they were buckled in, Sam tucked his arm around Rosie and pulled her to rest her head on his shoulder. "It'll only take about twenty minutes to get to the hotel, but why don't you have a nap in the meantime?"

Though her eyes fluttered closed, her body stayed taut and her mind raced over just how she should ask him to marry her. Should it come as a suggestion? Or should she reverse the roles and get down on one knee? Maybe she should buy a wedding ring for him tomorrow and ask him tomorrow night. No, enough waiting.

As they turned onto Forty Ninth Avenue, Rosie straightened. "Sam? While we were in the kitchen, Mama asked when we were planning to get married."

She didn't have to touch him to feel his body stiffen beneath her hand. Since the limo was going straight, he wasn't bracing himself against traffic. She glanced up and the Bambi-was-about-to-be-run-over-by-a-Mac-truck look on his face was like a knife in her chest.

CHAPTER FOUR

SAM SCHOOLED HIS FACE, hoping to hide his surprise, but he doubted whether he'd done it fast enough. Now what the hell should he do? Just went to prove that old adage about best-laid plans going awry was true.

Stall, boy. At least get her back to the hotel, where he could give her a perfect proposal. There was no way in hell he was doing it in the back of a damned New York cab, even if it was dressed up as a limo. "Can we talk about this later? Once we're back at the hotel. In private?"

Hurt filled Rosie's expression. "You don't want to marry me, do you?"

"No, yes," Shit. How the hell was he supposed to answer that? Frickin' double negatives. "I mean, yes, I want to marry you. I just don't want to do this here in the car."

Rosie leaned forward. "Driver, pull over. I'm getting out."

Shit on a stick. "Driver, don't pull over. Keep goin'."

Despite Sam's command, the chauffeur swerved to the curb. Rosie opened the door before the limo had come to a complete stop. Tires squealed and horns blew and traffic snarled around them and snow swirled into the once warm limo.

"Rosie, wait, let me explain." He clambered to the other side of the car in an effort to stop her climbing out. "Rosie, I want to marry you."

She batted his hands away. "You don't want to marry me. You just like screwing me."

With a curse, he told the driver to meet them a block down and if he hadn't convinced her to get back into the car by then, to follow until she did. By the time he turned to follow her, she'd marched at least a hundred yards ahead, weaving around the pedestrians, never stopping with her steady stream of curses in Spanish, cursing both him, his friends, his intentions, and the layer of snow that had accumulated during the day that sent the fancy heels she'd decided to wear sliding over the icy pavement.

Despite the gravity of the moment, he had to chuckle while he hurried to catch her. Back home she rarely reverted to Spanish, but after one day around her family, her accent was back with a vengeance.

After she'd launched into a long harangue about his parents' marriage or possible lack thereof, the invective finally slowed. Deciding she'd worked off her head of steam so she might actually listen to him, he closed the distance between them and touched her shoulder. "Rosie, hang on for a minute and listen to me. Please."

She stopped so quickly he nearly ran into her, took a breath then turned to face him. Snowflakes settled on her hair, bright white against the dark black, glistening in the street lights like a halo. God, she was so beautiful even when she was pissed at him.

When he opened his mouth to speak, she held up a hand to stop him. "No, it's fine. I thought we were somewhere we're not. Don't worry about me. I'll take the subway home."

Fuck that. Home was not on the New York City subway. Not anymore. Her home was in D.C. With him.

When she started to turn away again, he clamped his hands on her shoulders stopping her. "Rosie, listen to me. I want to marry you."

"Bullshit. You were ready to bolt when I mentioned it."

"You surprised me, that's all. I was fixin' to ask you in the hotel tonight. Honest." A flake of snow affixed itself to her eyelash and he brushed his thumb lightly over her eyes to remove it.

She caught his hand and held it away from her. "Sam, please. You don't have to pretend."

"I'm not pretending, baby."

"Then explain why you reacted the way you just did. Because I don't want you to propose to me because you feel obligated."

"Obligated? Damn it, Rosie. I've been trying to propose to you for the past three months. I was fixin' to propose to you during our trip to Hawaii but that trip got cancelled because of that mess with Chad. Then I figured I'd do it when he got back but then…"

"But then he got shot." The suspicion that had filled her voice faded. "Then you got called to San Francisco for that contract negotiation."

"Yeah, and by the time I got back, I figured I'd to take you to Paris this week and propose there, but then you said you made arrangements to come to New York for your mom's birthday and…damn it, Rosie, I didn't want to wait any longer and have anything else get in the way. But I also didn't want to propose in front your family."

What made him think anything about this would go smoothly, considering all the other times his plans had been interrupted? He took a deep breath and dove in, prepared for the worst while trying to stay positive, hoping for the answer he'd thought he'd expected the first time.

Screw it. His plans had just been shot to hell. He wasn't going to be able to propose in their suite at the Waldorf. There wouldn't be candlelight and flowers and champagne; he was going to have to do this on the corner of Forty Ninth and Third Avenue. Not the most romantic place for a proposal, but he was going to make damned well sure she believed him. Right here. Right now.

Ignoring the pedestrians skirting around them and the few who stopped to watch, ignoring the honking horns of the cabs, he lowered himself to one knee. The slush soaked through the fabric in an icy grip, not to mention the pavement was fucking hard. His knee was gonna hurt like a sonovabitch if he had to be down here for too long, but if he was going to do this, he was going to do it properly.

He reached into his coat pocket, pulled out the small blue box and flipped it open to display the ring, though he tried to shield it from onlookers. Last thing he needed was to get robbed. Though the locals strode past, not sparing them a glance, a half dozen tourists from the cameras slung around their necks stopped to watch, three of them holding up cameras, the rest cell phones.

"I love you, Rosalinda Maria Ramos. My life is better with you in it, with you beside me. You make me laugh, and I can't imagine life without you." Okay, that sounded cheesier than it had when he'd written it. "Will you marry me?"

Her eyes narrowed and he realized she was staring at the ring as if it were a coral snake, not a three-carat solitaire. "That's a Tiffany box, isn't it?"

"Yeah." Didn't all women want a Tiffany ring? He could have sworn that was the place those darned romance movies mentioned. "I picked it up during my last trip up here. I've had it sized for you and everything. I thought maybe you'd like to register at some of the stores while you're shopping with your mama tomorrow." After he'd made love to her all night.

The tip of her tongue darted over her lips. He'd never seen her so unsure. So why didn't she look convinced?

"Did you show that to my mother?"

"No." Had Carlos said something to his wife without him knowing? And if he had, or even if he hadn't, what had her mother said to Rosie to make her doubt him, damn it?

"Just to make it clear—I am not after your money or the size of the diamond you can buy me."

What the fuck? "I never thought you were with me because of money." Where had this come from? "You can say no, and I promise I won't be mad. You'll still have your job at Hauberk and I'll always take care of you, Rosie, no matter what happens between us."

It would hurt like hell not to see her but…wait a minute, he was proposing for fuck's sake, not breaking up with her.

He climbed to his feet, a sick feeling grabbing at his gut. The life he'd planned for them both, hell, even the plans he'd made for them tomorrow—accompanying her and her mother through the Fifth Avenue stores, pretending not to be interested when she registered them for wedding presents, spiraled into a dismal abyss that had his head pounding and his stomach ready to hurl.

Disappointed that they weren't given the expected "yes of course I'll marry you" response, the tourists moved on. Or maybe they were secretly laughing that she'd obviously turned him down.

Fan-fucking-tastic, ten to one, this would be on YouTube within an hour posted as "proposal gone wrong." Damned thing would probably go viral, and he'd never hear the end of it from the guys back in D.C. Or New York. Or any of his other offices, either. Which would be nothing compared to the dreariness of life without Rosie in it.

He touched his thumb to her chin and tilted it up until she met his gaze. "Rosie, I love you. I want to marry you. I want you in my life forever. I thought you loved me too."

"I do. I love you more than anything, but…" She stared across the street.

"But what?" He'd still been a kid when he'd learned a rejection always followed that damned word.

He could practically see smoke coming from her ears as the cogs turned inside. Was she worried that he was still in love with his old girlfriend, Jill? No, that couldn't be it. While he still grieved Jill's death, Rosie knew he'd finally been able to move forward. She'd accepted that long ago. Or was it something her mother had said to her while they were preparing dinner?

"What do you want, Rosie? Deep down inside? Do you love me enough to put up with all of my flaws?"

She pursed her lips, but he caught the slight upward tug at the sides. "Well, it's true that you do have a lot of bad habits. Like how you leave wet towels on the floor. And all that hair in the sink after you shave." Her nose curled. "Most women only have to deal with guys' beard hair. I had to contend with you shaving your head too."

He touched his hair, still not used to not feeling skin. "Is that why you wanted me to grow it out?"

"No." She shook her head, breaking eye contact. "I like you with a shaved head, but I wanted…" A blush rose up her throat. "I kind of like the idea of being able to bury my fingers in your hair. To hold you when you're…well, you know."

He raised his eyebrows as a blush crept up her neck. When you're...going down on her? The way he liked holding her by the hair when she went down on him? Well, wasn't that an interesting thought? And fucking sexy.

Except there was one question she still hadn't answered conclusively.

Once again, he lowered himself to one knee. Ah, shit on a stick, he could have at least moved out of the damned puddle. "Will you, Rosalinda Ramos, do me the honor of marrying me?"

She cradled his face in her palms and leaned her forehead against his. "Yes. Of course I'll marry you. I love you, Sam Watson. I'll even sign any prenup your lawyers want me to sign, just to shut up anyone who thinks I'm marrying you for your money."

He wrapped his arms around her waist and stood, lifting her off her feet. Not caring about the big shit-eating grin on his face, he carried her to the waiting limo. Once they were safely ensconced inside, he removed the ring from its box and slid it on her finger. Damned if it didn't look perfect. Satisfied, he pulled her onto his lap. "Now, who the hell thinks that you're with me because I have money? I want names."

"Mainly the women at the club. And sometimes the clients. Noelle."

Ah, that little gold digger. "I have never worried that you're with me because of my money. Ever. As for anyone else who thinks differently...well, I have a fucking big sharp stick they can sit on. I know you love me. And I love you." Unable to resist, he added, "Even with all your bad habits."

"My bad habits?" She sat up and folded her arms across her chest. "Name one."

"Shall we start with all those hair products you have cluttering up our bathroom counter?" Not that he'd trade them for anything. "Then there's your fondness for pickled eggs."

She poked him in the chest. "Hey, I like pickled eggs."

He grimaced. "They are disgusting. Just sayin'."

The limo pulled up to the curb on Park Avenue. The hotel's doorman opened the door, then politely stepped back, holding an umbrella over them as Sam climbed out.

Sam turned around and held out his hand, lacing his fingers with hers when she placed her palm in his. Hand in hand, he led her through the lobby with its magnificent chandelier, skirting the ornate clock in the middle of the aisle. As they passed, the concierge caught his eye and nodded discreetly.

Once Sam opened the door to their suite, Rosie's eyes widened at the profusion of red roses filling dozens of vases throughout the main room, plus the trail of rose petals leading into the bedroom. As he'd arranged, a bottle of champagne sat nestled in its silver ice bucket, fresh strawberries and pineapple piled around the chocolate fountain.

"It's beautiful." She reached out and plucked the closest rose from its vase, held it to her nose.

He snagged the remote to the stereo and pressed a button. As he'd planned, the first song from the playlist of romantic music he'd chosen for the evening serenaded her as she followed the trail of rose petals into the bedroom. The covers of their king-sized bed had been turned down, the red of the petals brilliant against the white sheets. The concierge and his staff had set up everything exactly as he'd asked.

It was perfect.

Except for the remnants of rice pudding in his lap and the frigid wet wool where he'd knelt in the street.

Ignoring both, he slid his arm around her waist and pulled her snug, moving them back and forth as the track changed to Diana Krall's The Look of Love.

"I love this song." Rosie snuggled against him, apparently unconcerned that he was probably getting her dress wet too.

"It's all in the details, Rosebud." He moved them around the room. Rosie relaxed against him as the track changed to an old slow Nat King Cole song. "I told you. I wanted to do it right. I wanted you to be surrounded by beautiful things when I proposed to you. I wanted you to have a beautiful memory of today, a perfect memory."

"Oh, Sam, I don't need perfect."

"No, but you deserve perfection. And I wanted to give it to you." Sam pressed a kiss to the top of her head. "You know, I even asked your father for permission this afternoon."

"You *dundo*." She leaned against his arms to stare up at him. "Even if he'd said no, I would have married you."

She moved like a dream against him, at one point lifting her leg from his knee to his hip in an erotic caress. He caught her leg beneath the knee before she could put it down, held her open against him.

Standing there, swaying to the music, he slid his hand down her leg to her ankle and held her in place while he ground his hips against her mound. A tidal wave of love surged through him, overwhelmed him.

She stared up at him, her eyes reminding him of earlier that evening when her nephew had climbed onto his lap. The tyke had the same eyes, the same thick fringe of dark lashes, even the same shape of her lips. At the time he'd been swamped with the thought that one day that might be his own child he'd hold, a child who would look just like Rosie.

"What?" she whispered. "What are you thinking?"

No words could describe what he felt for her. Instead of answering, he cradled her jaw, and captured her lips with his, tasting the wine they'd had after dinner. Reveling that she'd said yes, that they'd be together the rest of their lives, he sank deeper into the kiss. He flattened his palm over the small of her back and rotated his hips against her, eliciting a moan that had his cock jerking.

Did she realize she'd always dominate him, though she considered him her Dom? That pleasing her, fulfilling her needs was his motivation for everything he did?

With a deep moan, Rosie hooked her arms around his neck and lifted herself so she could wrap her legs around his hips. The craving to feel her skin against his took over his reasoning. He skimmed a hand up her spine and found the tab of her zipper, pulling it down to the small of her back. To his frustration, the pressure of their bodies kept the fabric between them. If his cock weren't still in his pants, he could take her, standing right here. Bury himself deep in the beautiful heat of her pussy. Press her against the wall and take her hard and fast.

No, he told himself. Tonight was for savoring. To show her how much he loved her. He'd not been able to give her a perfect proposal, those plans jettisoned back on Forty-Ninth and Third, but he could give her the perfect post-proposal evening.

Holding her tight, he twisted and laid her on the bed. Her arms and legs still clamped around him, he quickly realized he couldn't straighten.

"I've gotta get out of my suit."

Her arms loosened from their hold, but when he tried to stand up, she grasped his suspenders and held him in place. "Let me."

With the smile of an angel, she reached up to remove his tie and unbutton his shirt. His body trembling, demanding he take her right the hell now, he planted his hands on the mattress on either side of

183

her body and fought not to move. The touch of her fingers on his chest then his belly as she freed each button damned near undid him.

He closed his eyes as she loosened his fly, and blew a hard breath when her hand closed around his shaft. "Sweet baby Jesus, you gotta stop doin' that right now."

Despite her moue of discontent, she released him. Once he straightened, she knelt on the bed in front of him, her eyes dark with passion. His balls ached as she skimmed her hands over his chest, pushing his shirt down his arms, effectively pinning him.

It took all his reserve to stay still while her teeth scraped across his nipples, her breath hot on his flesh. His breath rasped and his heart pounded with each touch, each kiss, as her lips glided over his skin. Damned if the woman wouldn't be the death of him if she kept this up, but what a way to go.

Every inch of his chest and most of his belly had been caressed and savored before he couldn't stand it any longer. "Enough."

As Rosie sat back on her heels, Sam shrugged out of his shirt and let it drop to the floor. Moments later, he'd toed off his shoes and kicked off his pants.

"I can't decide if you're sexier in your suit or out of it," Rosie observed a mite too casually, her bottom lip caught between her teeth and a look of devilment dancing in her eyes. Her dress had slipped from her shoulders, revealing a black demi bra, her breasts luscious and full, her nipple tempting him behind its lacy cover.

He trailed one finger along her shoulder, over the curve of her breast to slip the tip beneath the lace. One simple tug freed her, eliciting a shiver and the already-hard nipple beaded tighter, though he doubted it was from cold.

Seconds later, he'd freed both breasts. He had to pause as his heart filled his chest, and his balls ached. "Wait here." He started to move away and then stopped. "Take off your dress, but leave your bra the way it is."

While Rosie slipped off her dress, Sam found the matches the concierge had placed on the mantel and went 'round the room, touching the flame to the candles they'd set up for the evening. He switched off the light and turned to face her, nearly swallowing his tongue at the sight.

The image of her kneeling, surrounded by rose petals scattered over the cream-colored silk of the comforter, of the black lace lifting her breasts like an offering to the gods, her dark eyes large and filled with promise, her lips slightly parted, plump from their kisses, burned into his memory as one of those single moments of perfection. Her hands rested loosely on her knees as she patiently waited, the ring on her left hand glinting, a physical declaration that she'd accepted him, wanted him. Loved him.

He cleared his throat against the lump that had formed. Not trusting his voice, he crossed the room and silently plucked the pins holding her hair in its rigid bun until the silken curls draped over his hand.

Rosie stroked the length of his arm, her touch a brand that caught his breath with each pass. "I love you, Sam."

Still unable to speak, he mouthed the words back to her and caught her hand and lifted it to kiss the soft skin on the inside of her wrist. He leaned over, gently pressing her back against the sheets, then paused to appreciate the picture she presented. She was so frickin' perfect lying there looking up at him, her lips curved into a smile, her legs parted by his legs, her cleft open and glistening, enticing and ready.

Though he'd tried to tell her before, he doubted she realized the effect she had on him. That all his doubts about himself, of his past and his future, had disappeared the moment she'd walked into his life. Now she'd be with him forever, his strength, his lover. His life.

She cupped the back of his head and touched her mouth to his. He sank into the kiss, trying to keep it easy and light or else he'd lose control, but she tasted like wine and sin and every fantasy he could ever imagine.

He'd braced his arms on either side of her head, careful not to crush her tiny figure, but he had to touch her or he'd surely go crazy. Shifting his weight, he freed one hand and cupped her breast.

"Sam, please." Rosie tightened her grip on his scalp, her fingernails adding a bite that drove him higher and harder.

Her breathy gasp filled his mouth, her body arched and rotated, the hard bud of her nipple grazing his palm in a maddening motion. So fucking perfect.

No reason to rush, he told himself as he banked the inferno threatening to incinerate him. He could spend all night kissing her if he wanted; after all, they'd have a lifetime together.

CHAPTER FIVE

IF SAM DIDN'T GET A MOVE ON, Rosie was going to flip him over and take charge. Yet there was something in his expression that slowed her frustration. He'd always been gentle, afraid to crush her, but tonight there was something different. Primal.

She'd had lovers that satisfied her before, but Sam…he touched parts of her no one else suspected existed, bared her secrets and accepted her without question. He understood her need to give someone else the power over her in the bedroom, where anywhere else she was a control freak, same as him.

She broke off the kiss and, cupping his head, lifted him so she could see his face. "I won't break."

"I know." He whispered the words as if he were afraid to speak. As if he couldn't. His eyes drifted closed and he laid his head in the curve of her shoulder, his breath hot on her skin. "I love you, Rosie. I wanted tonight to be perfect."

"It is perfect." He'd thought of everything. From the roses filling their suite with their heavenly scent, to the champagne in its silver bucket at the side of the bed, the rose petals, even the music softly playing every single love song he'd been able to find.

He nuzzled the tender spot beneath her ear while his hands roamed over her body. Finally he moved, his mouth following the path of his hands, as if greedy to establish his new status as fiancée. Future husband.

Husband. Wow. Not that he'd get all caveman on her and expect her to stop working or anything. They'd pretty much been living together as man and wife for almost two years now. But that word...husband. Yeah, it sounded right.

She skimmed her palm over the broad expanse of his back, his skin softly glowing in the flickering candlelight. Though others would mock her if she said it aloud, here in the privacy of their bedroom, all she could think was "hers."

The thought faded and her lids flickered closed when he laved one nipple with his tongue. He worshipped her breasts, teasing and tugging, until she quivered beneath him, aching to be filled, to be taken hard and fast.

He continued his path down her body, pressing kisses to her ribs, lingering over her belly button until he finally pushed her thighs wider. She couldn't stop her cry of pleasure when he canted her hips and put his mouth to her folds.

"God, I love how you taste." His voice was deeper than normal, filled with emotion. "It's like licking heaven and sin all at the same time."

Her eyes fluttered closed as he buried his face between her thighs once more, his beard rasping on the tender skin. His fingers dipped into her channel, while his tongue returned to tease her swollen clit.

He murmured again, nothing she could understand, but his words vibrated into her flesh until she couldn't think, couldn't see.

Her legs started shaking in an attempt to ward off her impending orgasm, even as her hands grabbed for his head, his shoulders, any part she could reach to drag him on top of her. "Inside me, please, Sam."

"Not yet." He lifted his head, his cheeks glistening with her juices. "Come for me, Rosie. Let me watch you."

He dipped his fingers deep into her sheath and touched that secret place until she shuddered around him, her entire body tightening in her release. Still he continued, driving her until nothing else existed, not the room, nor the world outside. The candlelight faded, the music muted along with the scent of the roses, until the only thing that existed was the pleasure Sam gave her.

When she finally came down, he slowed his movements. She whimpered at the loss of contact when he withdrew his fingers.

He stroked her thighs with his thumbs, towering over her, his eyes dark with lust. "God, you're so beautiful when you come."

As she panted in an attempt to get her breath and slow her pulse, he crawled back up her body, still holding himself off her with his elbows, stopping only when the head of his cock nudged her swollen folds.

His lips captured hers, his tongue parting them, her own taste filling her senses. She arched up to kiss him, but her movement changed the angle and the head of his cock breached her opening. She started to pull back, then stopped.

After watching him with Raphael...she filled her lungs and let it out slowly, aware of the commitment she was about to make. To ask him to make.

"Rosie," he warned around the kiss when she pushed his bare cock into her tight passage another inch. "We need a..." He dragged in a breath as he tried to think of the word. God, why was it so hard to think? She was driving him crazy. "Condom. We need a condom."

189

Her tongue darted out and licked the edges of her lips. A look of uncertainty entered her eyes. "I've been thinking. Maybe we could not use them tonight? Or…maybe for the next little while?"

He schooled his features to a blank expression while he considered the ramifications of her suggestion. Not using one, even once, meant… "You want to get pregnant?"

She nodded. "Yeah, I think I do."

Marriage and a baby at the same time? Whoa, this train was moving faster than a jackrabbit being chased by a hound dog. He thought back to playing with her nephew earlier and figured that's where this suggestion was coming from for her too.

"I mean," she continued, "we've been together long enough to know we'll work, right? And these days it doesn't matter if the bride's pregnant or not when she walks down the aisle. Plus, I'm in my thirties now and—"

"Whoa, you don't have to sell me on it." He blew out his breath in a long, slow blow. "Are you sure you want this? Because once we do, there's no goin' back. You get pregnant, and I'm in your life forever." There was no way in hell's half acre he'd walk away from her or any kid of his.

"That's why I'm sure," she said quietly, any trace of uncertainty vanishing from both her eyes and her voice. "Because I know you'll always be there for both of us. Because I love you, and you love me. What better reason?"

There were so many reasons not to have a kid these days, but the thought of Rosie swollen with his kid in his belly, of her cradling a tiny baby in her arms, breastfeeding it, of himself seeing part of himself staring back at him with Rosie's eyes. Then later, teaching the kid to catch a ball, or ride a bike…

Closing his eyes, he pushed fully inside her. The heat of her pussy incinerated him; the unfiltered flutters of her muscles against his bare flesh nearly pushed him over the edge without even moving.

He lifted himself up on his elbows and stared at the spot where his cock disappeared into her. Loving how her juices glistened on his cock, he withdrew slowly inch by inch. He gritted his teeth against the throbbing of her pussy around his shaft, squeezing his head as if her pussy was afraid to let him go. If she kept this up, he was going to be hard-pressed to give her gentle and soft, instead of taking her like a damned Neanderthal.

Her fingers raked his shoulders and clamped around his biceps, urging him to fill her once more. He damned near whimpered during the slow glide inside her heated channel. His eyes just about rolled back in his head when she tightened her muscles and locked him inside her. Sweet baby Jesus, there were no words to describe the sensation.

Encouraged by her fevered entreaties urging him deeper and harder, the slow pace he'd intended to set quickly fell by the wayside and soon his thrusts were fierce and frantic. Her fingernails dug into his skin in a delicious bite of pain that centered him as she rocked against him, heels digging into his ass. Her pussy throbbed with each pass then gripped his shaft, pulsing as she climaxed around him. His balls tight to his body, he stilled, letting her orgasm wash over him, only to find himself dragged into the vortex. A part of him registered each jerk of his cock, aware that with each spurt of his seed from his body to hers, he was truly inside her in every way.

Awed by the magnitude of the moment and the after-effects of her climax without the tiny, flickering pulses being muted by a condom, he lowered his head to the pillow beside her head. Once he finally slipped from her body and their breathing slowed, he tucked his arm beneath her shoulders and rolled onto his back, bringing her with him to rest on his chest. Rose petals that had stuck to her body and his fluttered around them, their scent filling the air.

"So, Mrs. Watson—" Damn, but he liked the thought of her having his name, as old-fashioned a concept as it might be, "—what do you think about getting married on the beach in Hawaii?"

Rosie tried to lift her head, her body bouncing on his as she chuckled when she failed. "Hawaii sounds heavenly. Or we could hold it in Puerto Rico. But we'd have to fly my whole family to wherever it's going to be if it's not in New York."

The where didn't matter much to him, as long as he got to put his wedding ring on her finger. He trailed his fingers along her shoulders and down the knobs of her spine, slowing at the small of her back to trace the outline of the butterfly tattoo that had entranced him since the first time he'd seen it peeking out above her jeans. "Maybe we can fly them out in Coop's private jet."

"That would be nice. Oh, and I'm not sure I want to be Mrs. Watson—that's your mom. Besides, I like the alliteration of Rosalinda Ramos."

"How about hyphenating it? Rosalinda Ramos-Watson." He rolled the name on his tongue experimentally. "It has a nice cadence to it."

"Or Rosalinda Watson-Ramos." She rolled over to poke him beneath the ribs where she knew he was ticklish. "You could always change your name."

"Rosalinda Watson-Ramos it is then." With a groan he lay back on the pillows and covered his eyes with his arm. "I can't believe I ended up proposing while kneeling in a puddle in the middle of the street. I wanted to give you a perfect proposal, one you'd never forget."

"Do you really think I'll forget today?" Straddling him, she sprawled across his chest and pulled his arm away from his face.

"And because I forgot to say it before, thank you for today, Sam. Thank you for giving up your plans of taking me to Paris and letting me visit my family. Thank you for the roses, and the music, and this suite. Thank you for wrecking your suit by getting down on one knee in a snow storm."

"It was worth it." Not that he'd point out that the suit was already a write-off thanks to Rosie's nephew dumping his pudding on it.

"You didn't have to go through all this, you know? I was never going to say no. In fact, I planning on asking you myself." She held her closed hand a foot above his chest, then opened her fingers, releasing a fistful of rose petals to cascade over him. "I don't need rose petals and fancy champagne or expensive hotel suites to know you love me. I just need you."

Cupping her face in his palms, he kissed the tip of her nose. "And I need you. That's why I wanted to give you a perfect proposal—because you're perfect for me."

He moved his hands down her back to cup her behind. "Now for part two of my plans for this evening..."

About the Author

Married to her college sweetheart and the mother of two sons, Leah is the only woman in a houseful of men—even their dog and cat are male. After a conversation with her eldest son about how he needed to follow his dreams, Leah decided she needed to take her own advice and make her dreams of getting published come true. She was thrilled when her first sizzling romance, *Private Property*, was published just eighteen months later. More contracts followed for the rest of her Hauberk Protection series, along with contracts from Harlequin's Carina Press for a series of Western romances.

Reviewers have awarded her books numerous Top Pick and Recommended Read designations. The reviewers at The Romance Reviews nominated *Tangled Past* as 'Best Erotic Ménage and More of 2011" and The romance Studio nominated *Private Property* for a CAPA award for "Best Erotic Romance of 2009", *Deliberate Deceptions* as "Best Contemporary Romance of 2011," *Hidden Heat* as "Best Romantic Suspense of 2012," and Leah herself has been nominated in the "Best Erotic Romance Author" and 'Favorite Author" categories.

For more information about Leah's books, visit her website at leahbraemel.com. You can also follow Leah on Twitter (@LeahBraemel) or find her on Facebook: Facebook.com/groups/LeahBraemelReaderGroup/ .

Don't miss the next steamy novel in the
HAUBERK PROTECTION series

HIDDEN HEAT

BY LEAH BRAEMEL

HIDDEN HEAT

Book 4 in the Hauberk Protection series

Wedding rings, babies, commitment? No thank you. Working for a company that's wall-to-wall, testosterone-fueled alpha males, Sandy Hallquist is in her element. By day, she's the picture of calm, cool efficiency. Off hours, her inner adrenaline junkie is off the chain.

His whole professional life has been all about being invisible, but nothing about Troy MacPherson is real, not even his name. It's the only way he can manage Hauberk's international offices while hiding his other career: assassin. But in one moment of weakness, Troy's carefully constructed mask begins to crack. Cracks that reveal his yearning for things he can never have. Family. Stability. Love.

Too bad they're the last things on Sandy's must-have list. By the time she realizes the heat between them will last a lifetime, his next mission could make him disappear from her life. Permanently.

A HIDDEN HEAT EXCERPT

HIDDEN IN THE SHADOWS, Troy allowed himself to picture Sandy shrugging out of her blouse. He imagined her shimmying out of her skirt, letting the fabric puddle at her feet to stand in front of him wearing only a scanty bra and perhaps, if he were lucky, a lacy thong. First thing he'd do would be to lick the freckles above her breasts and let the spice of her skin excite his taste buds. Then he'd suckle on her plump nipples until they were hard, maybe he'd let her feel his teeth on them. Once she was moaning her pleasure, he'd fill his palms with those full globes of her ass and part her legs, bury his cock deep inside her.

His breath hissed through his teeth when his fingers brushed the hard-on pressing against his fly in his attempt to create more space in his trousers. Talk about a glutton for punishment, letting himself fantasize about her. Now he was in desperate need of a little hand action to ease the ache in his balls. If he didn't get himself under control, he'd either spill in his pants or he'd be forced to seek the men's bathroom and find his relief in a stall.

The asshole stood. Good. He was leaving.

Shit. Sandy was standing too. And taking the asshole's hand. Three steps later Sandy slipped and Troy had seen enough. He slid from the booth, blocking their way before they could pass.

"I'll take her home."

Sandy huffed. "Troy, please."

"You know this jerk, Samantha?" Asshole's jaw tightened.

Now wasn't that interesting? Sandy hadn't given Asshole her real name. Troy sized him up. Manicured hands, not used to hard labor. The start of a pudge around the midriff. Desk jockey, at least lately. Not that it made him any less dangerous. The guy could be carrying a gun. Or a knife. Hell, he could be a former agent who'd been retired a few months too long but still retained the knowledge of how to incapacitate someone with his bare hands. "Yeah, she knows me. And I don't know you. So why don't you take a hike?"

"I don't think so." To his credit, Asshole placed himself between Sandy and Troy and stuck out his hand. "Mitch Young. And you are?"

Troy dropped his gaze to the outstretched hand and let it hang while he returned to meet Young's gaze. Okay, so maybe he wasn't a complete jerk. "McPherson. Troy McPherson."

Young's demeanor completely changed. He held up both hands and side-stepped Sandy. "Sorry, man, I had no idea she was married. She never said a word."

Married? Why the fuck would the asshole think he was Sandy's husband? Then again, who cared? Troy watched the man scuttle away before turning to Sandy, who glared at him. Rather than give her a chance to get away, he grabbed her wrist and hauled her out of the bar.

"Troy, stop it. You have no right to act like this." Despite Sandy's protests, she didn't struggle against his hold. "Will you slow down, please? I'm in high heels here."

He slowed but didn't stop until they were beside his SUV in the parking lot. "Damn it, woman, you don't have the sense of an overbred cocker spaniel, do you know that?" A spaniel with big blue puppy-dog eyes and soft wavy hair, lush curves and plump lips.

"Are you calling me a dog?" She flattened her hand against his chest and shoved him. At least she tried to shove him but ended up staggering backward herself.

"No." He crowded her against his SUV, trying to ignore the way her breasts brushed his shirt, or the way her lipstick glistened in the moonlight. *Focus, mate.* "Have you ever met this Mitch guy before tonight?"

"No, but who I decide to have a drink with is none of your business. I'll date who I want, when I want."

"Then you can get together with him another day, but I won't stand by and let you go off with a guy you don't know when you're drunk and not fit to make a decision."

"I'm not drunk. I was drinking virgin daiquiris, for Pete's sake."

"Sure as hell looked like it to me from the way you were stumbling your way out of the bar. Shit, did you take your eyes off your drink? Maybe he slipped you a roofie." He checked her eyes to see if she might be drugged only to have his hand slapped.

"Oh for heaven's sake. I'm not drunk and I'm not drugged. Someone must have spilled a drink, my heel slid. That's all. Besides, have you ever tried walking on four-inch heels? Do you know how hard it is, especially if some asshole is forcing you to keep up while he runs outside?"

He mentally took a step back, wondering if he had misjudged the situation. Then he made the mistake of looking at her again. Sparks of blue fire snapped out at him from those big puppy-dog eyes. Her chest rose and fell as she fought her anger. His body urged him to lower his head, to kiss her and capture her mouth with his, to draw some of that passion into his long-dormant soul.

A breeze whipped around the parking lot. She shivered and her nipples beaded beneath the silk of her blouse. As much as he wanted to be the one to warm her, he stepped back.

"You're cold."

"Because you dragged me out here without giving me the time to put my coat on, asshole."

Unable to argue her point, he took the jacket she clutched in one hand and held it open.

Her anger didn't disappear precisely but it was joined by questioning bemusement as she slid her arms into the sleeves. "Thank you. I'm still ticked off with you, you know."

Placing his hands gently on her shoulders, he turned her to face him. "Same goes. You need to be more careful about who you trust. There are some nasty types out there who will gobble a pretty girl like you up for a snack."

He couldn't resist playing with her collar as a way to cover his need to touch her hair. To touch her.

Her expression softened. "I know about the nasty types, Troy. I have to file the reports that agents submit, as well as sit in on the initial meetings with clients, which means I know exactly why they require bodyguards. I also volunteer with the Safe and Sound program. I've seen what those women have experienced before they made it to the shelter."

When she shook her head, her hair brushed the back of his hand in a soft caress.

All his protective instincts bristled that she could be put in danger from one of those abusers. "Tell me no one's been harassing you from there. None of the husbands who think it's easier to blame you than himself."

Her eyes closed briefly and a soft huff of exasperation escaped between her lush lips. "I'm fine. And stop trying to distract me about how you interfered back there. I'm still mad at you."

Smart girl. He caught a strand of hair and rubbed it between his fingers. "He wasn't your type."

"And you are?"

Not hardly. "No. I'm the big bad wolf. That's why you need to trust me that he wasn't right for you."

"What big eyes you have, Grandma?" Her lips compressed though the corners twitched as if she were trying not to smile. Then she tilted her head until her ear touched his thumb and the ground slid from beneath him. Why was it so hard to breathe from such a simple touch?

He gave in to impulse and lowered his head. Her eyes widened briefly, then they closed as he took the kiss he'd dreamed of for so long.

She tasted of strawberries and sugar. And everything good that must be found in heaven. Heaven became even more attainable when she slid her hands beneath his coat, around his waist and flattened them over his back, pulling him closer. He sank deeper into the kiss, her innocence a benediction, a cleansing of all his sins.

The Honda parked beside his SUV beeped and its headlights flashed, breaking the trance he'd fallen into. He couldn't remember a time when he'd ever been so reluctant to break off a kiss, but he forced himself to lift his head. To step back.

As the owner of the Honda cleared his throat and gestured to the door Troy was blocking, he took Sandy's hand and led her to the front of the car. She didn't say a word as she followed, but the look of complete trust she gave him wracked him with both guilt and desire. Her tongue darted out to moisten lips swollen from his kiss. In what seemed to be an unconscious gesture, she touched a hand to smooth the hair he'd managed to further tousle. Is this what she'd look like waking up beside him?

Stop it. She'd run screaming if she knew you killed an unarmed man this morning.

OTHER BOOKS BY LEAH BRAEMEL

HAUBERK PROTECTION

First Night (A short story)
Private Property
Personal Protection
Deliberate Deceptions
Perfect Proposal (a novelette)
Hidden Heat

TANGLE STORIES

Texas Tangle
Tangled Past

GRADY LEGACY SERIES

Slow Ride Home
No Accounting for Cowboys

OTHER STANDALONE STORIES

Feeding the Flames
I Need You for Christmas
Unashamed
Decadent (a short story)